Shelby's Ghost

by

Sarita Leone

Shelby's Ghost

Cover Art by *Debbie Taylor*

The Wild Rose Press, Inc.
PO Box 708
Adams Basin, NY 14410-0708
Visit us at www.thewildrosepress.com

Publishing History
First Fantasy Rose Edition, 2016
Print ISBN 978-1-5092-0987-3
Digital ISBN 978-1-5092-0988-0

Published in the United States of America

"Listen, we've got to talk.
I have things to tell you, and while I know they're not stuff your average Joe usually says, it's all on the level. Every single word of it. You've got to trust me."

She shook her head. "You're wrong about that, Joe whatever-your-name-is. I don't have to trust you. There's a house just the other side of the trees, and I could call the cops to have you picked up—hey, maybe I already called and they're on their way now. So why don't you just come clean? Who are you?"

A sigh. Mortals could be so tiresome. And this was just the beginning of what might be—although he hoped not—a long road.

If she only knew he didn't need to physically see her, or be near her, to know what she was doing, it would send her screaming into the trees again. So, he leaned back against the car. Summoned every ounce of other-worldly wisdom he possessed.

"We both know you didn't call the police. And even if you don't want to believe it, I've told you the truth." He paused, looking for the least-disturbing way to say this. But hell, there was no easy way so he shrugged. "My name is Joey Martinetti and… I'm a ghost."

Dedications

"From the outside looking in, you can't understand it.
From the inside looking out, you can't explain it."
~*~
For every Pi Delta Chi sister, past, present and future.
The bonds unifying us are eternal and priceless.
Special love to "the girls":
Brenda, Jeannine, Lynda, Maryanna, Penny and Sue.
I love you ladies more than words can ever say.
We totally took pledging and sisterhood to heart,
and it's carried us all far.
Here's to the next thirty-five years of love,
laughter and friendship!
~*~
For my wonderful parents.
You gave me wings
and encouraged me to soar.
I will be forever grateful for your love
and support.
~*~
And, as always, for Vito.
The love of my life,
he was wise enough to recognize
that when he married me
he gained a boatload of sisters-in-law,
Pi Chi style!

Chapter 1

It hadn't been a dream. The car was exactly where she'd found it yesterday, snugged up against the garage door as if it were a nursing infant latched to its life source. The bow still dangled from the rear-view mirror, its festivity the antithesis of her sudden foul mood. She stuck her tongue out at the car, barely resisting the urge to flip it the bird.

For a horrible moment, she considered walking down the drive onto Route 19 and hitching a ride to campus. Just jerk her thumb out, wait for a young mother or some righteous old dude to slow, roll down their window and offer a lift. Invite her to hop in—

"She's a honey, isn't she?"

Shelby nodded, glad she'd already pulled her tongue back inside her mouth. Plastering on a smile, she turned to her father. His designer suit, tie, and polished wing-tips effectively hid the true nature of the man. Banker on the outside, aging rebel within. It was sad society forced him to conform.

But everyone had to fit in somewhere, didn't they? Even when it meant exchanging bell bottoms and love beads for creased linen and Rolex.

Her father was not a man to be disagreed with, so she nodded. "She sure is."

It seemed to satisfy, so she let the comment suffice. In her mind, there were other adjectives she'd use to describe her birthday gift.

Her friends would have died to own the car. Literally, died. Compared to their battered beetles and funky Fords, it was a slice of automotive heaven.

The keys to the 1963 Shelby Cobra should've been in a museum with the car instead of in the purse of a twenty-year-old college junior—especially one who had been born the same year the car had been built. She had no desire to own either the car or its keys. Sure, it was sweet, streamlined, and shiny. The paint and chrome gleamed. All the more reason, in Shelby's opinion, to keep the thing safely out of harm's way. And out of her less-than-proficient driving hands.

Damn it. Why couldn't she have gotten a Pinto or some hunk of junk for her birthday, the way other kids did? No one in their right mind should present a car like this to anyone.

But there was no way her father would've given her something comparable to what her friends owned. He'd be the first to say he'd worked too hard to let his daughter drive something ordinary.

Donald Carmichael had made a killing on oil stocks when the economy was at its peak. And he'd had the foresight to pull out of the market just before the recession hit in December '73. While others lost their savings, he waited for the upswing, sitting on the family nest egg until the opportunity to reinvest presented itself. As a result, he was worth more than anyone suspected. More than he would admit, even to himself.

The management position at Sheffield Trust provided well enough that the egg need never be touched. Not even to pay for the gleaming blue roadster before them.

Granted, the car had been a steal. Well, almost a steal. And it'd had to be redone. Or rebuilt. Or refurbished. Whatever an old, neglected car needed was what had happened. She didn't care what it had taken to make it run and shine again. If it still languished, abandoned and forgotten, in a barn in upstate New York where it'd been discovered, she'd be much happier.

She hadn't even driven the thing, and she already hated it.

Her father put an arm around her shoulders and pulled her close. Since her mother's death, he'd been even more reserved than was his norm, so this demonstration of affection was unexpected. She leaned against him, knowing all-too-soon he'd pull away, placing the barrier he'd built between them up again long before she was ready.

They'd been prepared to lose her mother. The progression of ALS had made it horribly clear there was no surviving the disease long before the final days drew near. Shelby had been ready for that—or as ready as anyone could ever be—but she hadn't dreamed she'd lose her father, too. The fun-loving man she'd known her whole life was gone, swept away with her mother's dying breath. It was almost as if the life had gone out of him, leaving behind a shell that walked, talked and seemed alive but was, in actuality, hollow.

It almost hurt more to watch him be a walking dead man than it did to visit the cemetery to place flowers on her mother's grave.

Donald straightened his arm, motioning to the car.

"A car that shares your name. Now that's something, isn't it?"

She nodded, wishing she'd been named Linda or

Susan. "It sure is…something."

"Bet you'll be the envy of the university. Just be sure to park it way from the VW Bugs and rust buckets, okay? Don't want any dents in it."

The thought of being the "envy" of anything, anyone or anyplace made her tummy flip flop. Just riding down the street was going to garner attention, something she hated.

"I…ah, I…" How to explain she'd rather have a root canal without sedation than drive the thing?

"It's okay, honey. Just park on an angle in across two straight spaces. Don't worry about getting a ticket. If you do, I'll pay it. And I'll give Dean Thompson a call this morning, just to let him know your birthday gift might need a little extra leeway. We're Alpha Tau from way back, so a brother-to-brother favor won't be a problem."

Alpha Tau brothers and Omicron Kappa Pi sisters, both old and new, were family. Shelby had pledged her freshman year—not because she wanted to be in a sorority, but because her mother was an alumna who loved her sisters so much she'd been buried wearing her gold Omicron pledge pin. The sorority had been a godsend to Shelby, holding her up when she would have stumbled.

God forbid, the other sisters found out Dean Thompson was giving her preferential treatment. Or worse, if the head-bangers got wind of it. They'd surely have a blast making fun of her. Any excuse to disrespect a so-called "preppie" was worthwhile to the artsy crowd who didn't hide their derision of Greek life.

"Dad, no. Please, don't do that."

Shelby shifted her backpack from one shoulder to

the other, careful not to wrinkle her freshly-ironed oxford button-down. Baby blue today, to match the ribbon in her hair and polish on her fingertips. Later, just before the rush party, she'd pull on her Omicron Kappa jersey and add a navy ribbon to her hair. Blue and white were easy to coordinate, although, like most of the other sisters, she wished the founders had chosen a more feminine palette for their official colors.

"It's no trouble." His gaze never left the car, sweeping from front grille to rear fender in a lover's caress. "Butch will be happy to help."

Butch, the fraternity nickname given so long ago still carried to this day. It was hard to imagine the portly, spectacled dean being called Butch. Or like her father, being young and wild. But Alpha Tau had a reputation that spanned decades, so the old don't-judge-a-book-by-its-cover motto seemed applicable.

"It's not that. It's just…"

He knew her too well to not sense her discomfort. Or her attempt to hide the truth.

Turning, he met her gaze. "It's just what?"

"I, ah…"

"What is it, honey? I love that car, and I know you do, too. I'm sure Butch might be able to give you a private parking space. That's what brothers do, take care of each other—and their nieces-by-Greek-life."

There was no polite way to tell the man who would have given her the moon that she was embarrassed by his gift. That the very notion of driving it made her hands clammy. That she would have gladly traded for a bus pass.

So she shrugged.

"You're right. I was just worried the dean might

not want to give me special treatment."

"Hey, that's the way the world works. One hand washes another." He tapped his chin. It was a thinking gesture she knew so well, and loved because he had no clue he did it. When he turned to face her, he caught her watching him. "You *do* like the car, don't you?"

She forced the edges of her lips upward. "Who wouldn't?"

The smile that lit his eyes from within was well worth the lie. Before her mother got sick, he'd smiled all the time. Now, any sign of joy was a rare event.

"That's my girl." He leaned down, picked up his black leather briefcase, and checked his watch. Before the sleeve on his jacket slid back into place—and without any farewell kiss or wave—he strode toward his car. The sensible navy-blue sedan was as sedate as his suit, and probably no better liked than the job or life he now led. "Happy birthday again—enjoy the car. And remember, park it away from anyone else until I talk with Butch."

Without a backward glance, he pulled out of the driveway.

For a long moment, Shelby didn't move. The car seemed to mock her, its glossy paint such a contrast to her plainness.

"Flash meet frump." She took the keys from her bag. "You may want to speed along, but we're going to take it nice and slow. And if we're lucky, we won't end up wrapped around a tree because I hit the wrong pedal."

Chapter 2

First lesson from the Cobra? Not all stick shifts were created equal.

Shelby learned to drive on a stick so it never occurred to her that there would be such a discrepancy between cars. Nothing she'd done in her mother's Dodge prepared her for the raw power suddenly at her fingertips.

Thankfully she'd managed to get out of the neighborhood without grumpy old Mr. Sawyer from down the block spotting her. At least, she didn't think he'd seen her. Heard her, maybe. The big Ford 427 engine roared, despite her inept gear shifting.

Next Door Dude—thusly named because she didn't have a clue what his real name was, even though they'd lived side by side for the past couple of years, looked up from the tangled flower bed beside his mailbox when the car hiccupped at the end of her drive. A slow wave, and a headshake, as she popped the clutch.

If there had to be a witness to her ineptitude, she'd take the dude over the grouch, any day.

Her first class, Psychology of Adolescent Behavior, wouldn't begin for two hours. She had planned to stop by the frat house on her way to campus, just casually peek in to see who was around. And maybe, who needed a ride.

Actually, she was hoping to catch a few minutes

alone with Turner, her on-again-off-again boyfriend. They'd dated casually for a year, but he'd pinned her at the last Yule Ball so now she was more interested in what—and whom—occupied his free time.

Turner wasn't known for his faithfulness. But that was the past, she reminded herself. They'd pledged their love, one for the other, and that had to mean something. Didn't it?

Well, now her plan for the frat house drive by was blown. She'd be damned if she was going to make a spectacle of herself screeching to a stop outside the big red brick building. It was better to take the car for a spin, give herself a chance to get used to the thing.

The idea that she might be able to refuse the gift had vanished when her father smiled. Disappointing him was not something she would do if she could help it.

The car was actually comfortable. Cozy, even. The interior was simple. Just two form-hugging black leather bucket seats. A flat-panel dashboard. An extra gauge or two that she didn't know anything about, but otherwise it was all fairly normal.

The low-slung aluminum body wasn't much to see from the driver's seat. Sure, the hood was there, with its backward latches that lifted the panel from the front rather than near the windshield, but it wasn't nearly as impressive as surveying the entire automobile from outside. Then, the full effect of its deep blue, sparkly paint and the wide, white racing stripe running up the center of the hood truly dazzled.

Behind the wheel? It wasn't a clunker, but unless she pressed the gas, it was just a car.

What was it about cars that made men so hot? She

couldn't count the number of times talk in the fraternity house had gone from social to serious, all over carburetors, mufflers, and the ever-popular-and-widely-disputed engine size debate. Honestly, cars and trucks flipped men's minds even more quickly than baseball or football did.

Although as she drove further from traffic, she had to admit the little automobile did handle well.

I'll drive it until Dad forgets about it, she thought.

She steered into a curve. The road out of town was deserted, so she gave herself permission to stomp on the gas a bit.

As if lifted off the asphalt by angels, the car flew. No wonder the Cobra's big claim to fame had been on a racetrack. Even the street version bumped up the whole driving experience.

If she wasn't worried what the girls at the house or the fraternity brothers would say—and how terribly they'd tease her for owning such a wild car—she would have considered keeping it. But they would rag her, and she wasn't keen on smiling when she wanted to cry. Lord knows, she did enough of that, between her mother's passing and Turner's roving ways.

No, she'd have to just wait her father out. Then, trade it for something sensible. A Dart or a bug. Maybe a van so she could help her sorority sisters move stuff between events. It was hard smashing every paddle and composite into their cars. A set of wheels with a big backseat would be the thing to get.

Lost in thought, Shelby forgot to downshift as she took a corner. And she was going too fast to stay in her lane. Had there been someone heading her way, it might have been messy. Very messy.

One way to get rid of the car, she thought with a tiny smirk.

"Listen, babe, pay more attention to the road. You nearly creamed us on that turn."

Her head whipped around. The guy in the passenger seat was drop-dead gorgeous, in his mid-twenties with longish black hair that curled at the ends where it brushed his collar. The eyes that held her gaze captive were startling. The deep chocolatey brown irises flecked with gold were so compelling she could not look away.

Or breathe. The breath she hitched when he spoke was still lodged in her lungs.

"Watch the road!" He reached across the tight space between them, so she jerked the wheel to the left, away from his outstretched hand.

She looked up in time to see an old-fashioned Woody station wagon coming directly for her. Swerving even more, she managed to avoid a collision but got a blast from the other's horn that was so long, loud and angry it could have woken the dead.

No time to think about the other car or the man beside her. Or even about waking the dead. Instead, Shelby fought to regain control of the car, praying in the seconds where she bumped across the shoulder and onto an expanse of grass bordering an apple grove that she wouldn't be killed.

Shit! Shit, shit, shit!

She stomped on the brake. The transmission whined, then stalled. The only sound was the ticking of the cooling engine and the hammering of her own heart. Both sounded loud in her ears and mingled with her shuddering breaths.

"What are you trying to do? Kill yourself? Wreck the car?" He was much less affected than she was, able to find words while she struggled to find a coherent thought.

One hard tug had the door handle up and a shoulder shove sent the driver's side door flying open. She scrambled out onto the grass. It was almost a tumble from the vehicle, a most unladylike and definitely immodest move that no Omicron Kappa would ever intentionally execute, but hey, it got her out of the car.

She stumbled, nearly turning an ankle. Her loafers had slick soles. Fine for campus but not so great for running.

It was foolish to run from her own car. The trespasser should be the one hot-footing it! What the hell was she thinking? She stopped. Pivoted.

The man sat on the hood of her car as calmly as if he were Humpty Dumpty, completely unsuspecting of the fall he would eventually take. His jeans were dark blue denim, cut tight across the thighs and pegged at the ankles. Black biker boots concealed his feet, which hit the ground even with his butt on the bullet-nose.

It hit her that his ass must be made of asbestos, because that big V-8 engine had to have heated up the hood.

"Who are you?"

A stupid question. She realized it the moment it was out of her mouth, but there was no recalling it so she planted her feet and put her hands on her hips. Look imposing, she thought. The beige pleated khakis showed her figure to its best advantage.

He noticed. His gaze swept down her body, then up

to her face. A long, low whistle cut the morning quiet.

"You're a sight for sore eyes." His gaze flicked down again, lingering on her thighs. "Those trousers look painted on. Be still, my aching heart…"

Was this a hallucination? Could there be gas fumes in the car, clouding her mind? Residual effects from the one hit she'd taken off Jim Hornsby's bong at the frat mixer last month?

Hallucinations didn't stare at a woman's boobs. Not that she had any experience with delirium or even recreational psychedelic drug use, but she was pretty damn sure phantasms didn't zero in on cleavage.

"My eyes are up here." Time to take the upper hand, show him who was in control. She'd taken a self-defense for women course last semester. If she had to, she'd bash his balls with the heel of her shoe. That'd have him singing the blues instead of leering at her.

He met her gaze with a slow, sexy smile. She had to admit, a whole legion of butterflies fluttered deep in her gut. Whether from shock or lust was hard to tell.

"I saw those gorgeous eyes. Aquamarine, so true and clear they would make a sailor weep. Bedroom eyes."

Normally she would thank someone for commenting favorably on her looks, but this wasn't a casual conversation. They weren't hanging out at the Rathskellar or attending a rush party. It wasn't even a football game, where Greeks mixed with the jocks so well they almost forgot they usually attended different events.

No, this was a field, off the two-lane road that, as she scanned it, was completely empty.

Great. She was alone with this guy.

Thank God for the ball-crushing move. If he took one step closer, she'd go all Bruce Lee on him. Kick first, ask questions later. Or never, depending on how out of commission she rendered him.

"How did you get in my car?" She fisted her hands, keeping them on her hips. Hopefully he'd get it that she meant business.

He looked at her for a long, silent moment. Then he slanted his head back, closed his eyes and said, "Gorgeous day, isn't it?"

Was this guy for real?

"Hey—I asked you a question. How did you get in my car?" Shock had turned to frustration. She nearly shouted at him.

One eye opened, and his head tilted ever-so slightly to catch her gaze. It seemed he wasn't going to answer, but after nearly a full minute without either of them blinking, he sighed, opened the other eye, and lifted his shoulders, as if by way of explanation.

"Well? How did you get in my car?" She scowled and was about to take a step closer when he answered.

"Here's the thing: It's *my* car." He held up a hand, traffic-cop style, when she opened her mouth. "I died within sight of this Cobra twenty years ago."

Chapter 3

It was one of those perfect northeastern fall days when there's no hint of the winter brutality lurking just on the horizon. A few more weeks, at most, before all the yellow, red, and orange maple leaves were on the ground. A month, maybe, before the first snow flurries sent everyone to closets for mittens, scarves and coats.

Shelby sat on the ground beneath a dwarf apple tree whose branches were so heavy with ripe fruit they nearly touched the earth. Apples were scattered all around her. A few had been partially eaten by deer but most were intact. She picked one up and rubbed it on the leg of her pants.

Nothing prepared her for this moment. Not her mother's illness and death. Not her father's grief-induced distance. Not the loss of the loving, stable family she'd thought to hold onto into her old age. Not being Haverhill High's Homecoming Queen. Not even serving as president of Greek Council last semester. Nothing—none of it or anything else, for that matter, gave her the wisdom or experience to deal with what had just happened.

Correction. What was *happening*.

She had left the man—apparition, ghost, hallucination?—behind with the Cobra. For all she knew, he'd driven it away by now. She could be stranded in the apple orchard, all her books and

14

personal items in her purse and backpack stolen. Lost forever.

The only thing she'd miss was the photo she carried in her wallet. It had been taken when she was four years old, and she had ridden an elephant at a local fair. Both of her parents were astride the massive animal's back; Mother and Father behind her, his arms around them both. They all had huge smiles on their faces, and aside from it being such a perfect, spontaneous, joyful moment, it was an event she remembered clearly. As if it were only yesterday. Maybe it was her earliest memory, even.

The car and everything else could be replaced. But the photograph? If it was lost, it would break her heart.

"I'm finally losing my mind." It wasn't her habit to talk to herself, but if ever there was a time to begin a new, and possibly sanity-saving, habit, this was it. "Too much stress. Not enough fun. Class overload. Romance underload."

Now she sounded like Dr. Seuss, so she closed her mouth and took a slow, deep breath. Her heart still raced inside her chest and her hand, the one that wasn't wrapped around the Macintosh, shook.

What had the yogi said in the class she took last break?

In through the nose, out the mouth with only serenity left behind.

She tried. Pulled the sweet smell of apple in through her nose. Held her breath, willing her lungs to expand to hold all the oxygen-rich air she'd filled them with. Then, a long, unhurried exhale, releasing all the negative energy.

Why had she stopped yoga practice when the class

ended? It was silly, really, since the cloak of calm that covered her almost instantly had to be worth the effort of daily practice.

What you live, you become. The yogi, an energetic single mother with the curliest red hair this side of Bozo, had repeated the mantra so many times during the short sessions.

Shelby believed it, although she hadn't made any progress toward living differently or an effort to change.

"One step at a time." Next Door Dude had a t-shirt with the motto emblazoned across the chest. He wore it so often it was nearly ragged, but the five words had to mean something to the guy. If they worked for him, they might work for her, too.

The apple was still in her right hand. She looked down, saw its gleaming skin. Lifting it to her lips, she took a bite. Chewed. Swallowed. Then, another bite.

Big whoop—so now I'm twenty, she thought as she ate.

Shouldn't life's post-teenage years be better than this?

Practically on her own. Only one year of college left. Now the owner of a car which shared her name as well as her disfavor. A sorority she loved. A job she didn't mind.

And a boyfriend who was…well, Turner Walker was like that story her mother used to tell her about the little girl with a curl. When she was good, she was very, very good. And when she was bad, she was horrid. That about summed up the guy's personality. When they were on the same wavelength, things were great between them. But there were times—too many times to count, actually—when the apple cart overturned and their relationship took a beating.

Thinking about Turner wasn't going to solve the problem at hand. Just beyond the trees, hopefully her car waited. With her stuff.

And, if she were very lucky, the guy would be gone.

Although…

Shelby sat back against the smooth tree trunk and turned the apple in her hand. One side had been eaten down to the core. She began on the other, each crunch of fruit between her teeth giving her time to consider the guy she'd run from. He was easy on the eyes, from what she'd seen. Handsome, in a careless—but not sloppy—kind of way. The jeans were tight in all the right places; just remembering how they'd hugged his thighs made something heat way down low in her own trousers. She sighed, took another bite, and thought about the eyes. They were like none she'd seen on anyone—man or woman—before. There was a depth to them, as if someone could fall into them and be lost forever.

"Too much punch." She shook her head, threw the core across the orchard, and scowled. How could she be so silly?

The punch at last night's frat party must've had more alcohol in it than the guys said, because her brain was cloudy all these hours later. It was the only explanation—that the punch was more rum than juice— that would explain her morning.

She pushed to her feet, wiped the grass off her behind, and walked toward the road. This craziness had to end, and now. There was too much on the schedule for her to give in to insanity. Another time, perhaps, but not today.

She reached the last row of apple trees. Ducking beneath the lowest branches of a dwarf Fuji, she came in sight of the car. Thankfully, the blue-and-white roadster was exactly where she'd left it.

So was the handsome stranger.

Oh, shit.

Chapter 4

Joseph Sebastian Martinetti had been one of the so-called "bad boys" of the neighborhood when he was alive.

He roared through the quiet streets on his '47 Knucklehead at all hours of the night. Working bar jobs, both behind the counter and banging the ivories on stage, didn't make for respectable hours. Sure, he could've gotten a bend-over job in the coal mine, like some of the guys who hung out at the local dive, Chester's, or signed on to sell insurance door to door like his pal Muncie.

Neither prospect appealed, and the truth was, he made more at his disrespectable gig pulling drafts and hammering out tunes. It gave him enough money to keep the Harley in gas so he could run around—day and night. It paid his mother's mortgage and electric bills, as well as for the washing machine he'd bought her for Mother's Day. He'd even been able to buy his dream car, the Cobra, from a hot rodder who suddenly found his girl in the family way. When it came to marrying a woman and caring for a kid, there didn't seem to be any room for the bullet on wheels, so Joey was more than happy to take it off the other guy's hands.

He wondered what ever happened to the guy. Or his girl. And the kid.

The baby must be just about Shelby's age. The

realization hit him that he'd been dead long enough to miss all the early steps in a person's life: babyhood, childhood, teenage rebellion. Damn, but it didn't seem fair.

The difference between BD and AD time was vast. Before Death, time sped by. His life was a blur, a jumble of memories and events that felt crammed into one teeny, tiny space in his mind. After Death, well that was another story. Time, if it was actually the same sort of hours, days, months, and years experienced by mortals, crawled. Absolutely crawled. Sometimes, it felt as if it moved backward.

He'd waited an eternity for someone to buy the Cobra. Twenty years living time translated into an eon in dead time.

Forget about that, he thought. This is here and now—and I've got a chance to redeem myself.

The lady was a looker. That much was in his favor. If he had to be relegated to the passenger seat of his own car, it was better to see a hot chick instead of some old gaffer behind the wheel.

How to help her, though? She was young. Beautiful. Had a father who loved her enough to plop down the moolah to not only pay for, but restore the Cobra. From what he'd picked up from the father-daughter conversations he'd overheard, she went to college. A girl with such gorgeous green eyes and a figure that would turn a choir boy into a wolf had to have a boyfriend somewhere.

What could she possibly be missing that he could perhaps get for her? No, that wasn't right. That was his "old" way of thinking, the take-what-you-want attitude that made him so much a rogue that "nice" girls refused to date him. He had to shape up, now that he was dead. If that wasn't a hoot, he didn't know what was.

If he'd toed the line when he was alive, he might not be dead.

Damn.

Too late now, he reminded himself.

The chick was coming through the trees. He could've followed her but figured she might do better with some time alone. Hell, she'd just driven off the road in a sports car with a ghost—who wouldn't need a minute—or ten—after that?

She stopped. Stared. Shook her head.

Ah, he got it. She thought she'd lost her mind.

Welcome to the club, girlie. I've felt that way for just about two decades now.

He waved. Smiled.

Called out. "I'm glad you came back. I was beginning to worry about you."

He wasn't, but things might go better if she viewed him as a compassionate sort.

She walked slowly toward him, and he saw again that she was exceptionally pretty. Long, gold-blonde hair pulled back in a blue ribbon. Those striking green eyes. Creamy complexion and bow-shaped lips. His gaze traveled lower, sliding over the curves that were in all the right places. A stunner, all right.

He wasn't the only one taking a good, long look. Her gaze moved down his body, lingering low, which was hot. Women in his time weren't that bold. She lifted her gaze, a tiny smile raising the corner of her upper lip in a way that would have sent his blood boiling, had his blood still been hot in his veins.

She stopped about ten feet from where he leaned

on the hood of the car.

"Who are you?" Her voice, now that she wasn't screeching, was pure honey. Sweet and soft, exactly the way a man wanted a woman to sound.

Turning on the charm, he placed an arm across his midsection and bowed slightly. "Joseph, but my friends call me Joey."

He straightened to find her studying him. The stare could've bored a hole in his skull, it was so penetrating, but he didn't flinch. The character of a man came through in many ways, including how he didn't back down from a confrontation. She might be small, but she was mighty—and he wasn't stupid enough not to realize it. So, he kept his wits and the smile, and let her squint and stare.

Finally, she crossed her arms. He couldn't help himself; he dropped his gaze when the action pushed her breasts high. High enough, even, that a bit of cleavage and a strip of lace showed at the opening of her blouse.

Blouse? Now that he looked more closely at it, it looked like a man's shirt more than a woman's blouse. What had happened in twenty years to make women wear slacks and button-down shirts? Where were the skirts, dresses, and lacy blouses he remembered? And stockings—where the devil had stockings gone?

"My eyes are up here." The words dripped ice.

He met her gaze. "They are, and they remind me of emeralds."

She ignored the flattery. "So, Joseph-my-friends-call-me-Joey, what are you doing in my car?"

He plowed a hand through his hair. It'd been longish for his time, hitting his collar when most guys had buzz cuts. He hadn't cared what people thought, didn't seek anyone's approval, so had eschewed the clean cut in favor of something that blew in the breeze when he opened up the Knucklehead.

He hoped it didn't count against him now. The odds already weren't in his favor.

"Listen, Shelby—"

She cut him off as fast as a hot knife slices through butter.

"How do you know my name?" The demand took some of the sweet from her tone.

"I know a lot about you."

Her eyebrows went so high on her forehead they nearly disappeared beneath the fringe of bangs.

Damn, he'd stepped in it. He'd have to be more careful. Remember why he was here. Focus.

And stop pissing her off. Or scaring her—that wasn't good, either.

He tried another angle, putting one hand out, palm up so she could see he meant no harm. "Listen, we've got to talk. I have things to tell you, and while I know they're not stuff your average Joe usually says, it's all on the level. Every single word of it. You've got to trust me."

She shook her head. "You're wrong about that, Joe whatever-your-name-is. I don't have to trust you. There's a house just the other side of the trees, and I could call the cops to have you picked up—hey, maybe I already called and they're on their way now. So why don't you just come clean? Who are you?"

A sigh. Mortals could be so tiresome. And this was just the beginning of what might be—although he hoped not—a long road.

If she only knew he didn't need to physically see her, or be near her, to know what she was doing, it would send her screaming into the trees again. So, he leaned back against the car. Summoned every ounce of other-worldly wisdom he possessed.

"We both know you didn't call the police. And even if you don't want to believe it, I've told you the truth." He paused, looking for the least-disturbing way to say this. But hell, there was no easy way so he shrugged. "My name is Joey Martinetti and... I'm a ghost."

Chapter 5

Shelby's attempt to leave her uninvited visitor behind failed miserably. She walked past him, watching from the corner of one eye as she neared the car in case he tried to grab her. He didn't, so she opened the driver's side door, climbed into the seat, and placed her fingers around the key that still dangled from the ignition.

Before she turned it, she looked at him through the windshield. He hadn't moved, not one inch, from the leaning position against the hood. She raised an eyebrow, his only warning to remove himself from her car. When he didn't budge, she brought the engine to life, put it in reverse, and backed over the grass.

Her shifting skills still weren't great, but she managed to get the car in gear and headed toward the university. She'd wasted enough of the morning already and would have to scramble to make up for the lost time.

"Did you think you could leave me behind?"

She jerked the wheel, nearly driving off the road a second time.

It would have been too easy to just drive away. It almost made her smile at her own foolishness, thinking her life could be so simple that her problems would just disappear in the rear-view mirror.

The signal light clicked as she pulled onto the

shoulder.

"Get out."

The smirk that turned good-looking to rock star material sent a jolt of electric lust up her spine. She ignored it, setting her lips in a straight line that made her look—she hoped, anyway—fierce.

"Listen, babe, it doesn't work that way."

"I'm not your babe." She gripped the steering wheel so tight her fingers hurt. "Now, get out."

She would have reached across and opened the door but that meant touching him, and so far she'd avoided that. He was definitely tempting, but it seemed best to keep some space between them—even in the tiny car.

"I told you, it doesn't work that way." He grinned, ran a hand through his hair. "You could be my babe, you know. You'd like it, I promise. I don't want to toot my own horn, but I do know how to treat a lady, and you're one fine specimen of womanhood. So if you've got a mind to, we can—"

"*Get out!*"

She hadn't meant to scream, but hey, everyone had a breaking point and she'd just reached hers.

"Whoa, babe—"

"I'm NOT your babe!"

"Damn, you're really riled up. I knew you'd be pissed, but this—"

"Out!"

"I keep telling you, I can't."

Her heart beat so hard she was surprised it didn't burst through her skin. The last time she'd been this upset had been…never. Not even when she'd caught Turner with the Epsilon Phi Farrah Fawcett wannabe behind the concession stand at the Longview Drive-In. She'd been upset, sure, but nowhere near this heart-pounding frustration.

Hurt and frustrated were clearly two different emotions.

"Okay, if you won't get out on your own, I'll take you to someone who'll help you out."

She pulled onto the road. Thankfully, she had to pass campus security on the way to the parking lot.

They rode in silence for a few miles.

"I know what you're thinking." When she didn't respond, he went on. "You figure that you can take me to the cops, or some version of them at your school, and they'll be able to eject me. Forcibly, probably—which you wouldn't mind witnessing, I'm sure. After all, I've been a royal pain in your ass."

There was nothing he'd said that she didn't agree with so she kept driving. Besides, she'd decided to pretend he wasn't there.

Campus was only a mile or so up the road. Traffic was heavier here, but there were no stop signs or lights, so she didn't have to sweat the whole shifting-without-grinding thing. One bright spot in the otherwise-crappy morning, at least.

"I haven't seen this many people in…well, longer than I want to admit."

She shot a glance his way. His attention was on the action outside the car, so she let her gaze linger on his profile for an extra second or two. It hit her that he had the "chiseled features" she so often read about in the classics in lit classes.

She wanted to remain aloof, but she couldn't hold her curiosity in check. "When was the last time you were…um, in a crowd?"

Without taking his gaze from the street scene, he shook his head. "Too long ago."

"Are you from around here?"

"Around here, yes. But not in a long time."

Now was the chance she'd waited for. "Are you sure there's not someplace I can drop you off? A friend's house, maybe? Or Main Street, where all the shops are? It wouldn't be any problem at all, really." She forced a friendly tone.

A masculine chuckle sent gooseflesh along her arms. "It would be more of a problem than either of us are equipped to handle, I'm afraid."

"I don't mind at all. Just tell me where you want to go, and I'll take you there."

They'd reached the town proper. At the intersection of Main and Cedar, she stopped to let a group of toddlers herded by three harried-looking preschool teachers meander from one sidewalk to the other. Their progress was slow, which gave her time to mentally practice the shift sequence.

"I wish it were that simple." As soon as the kids cleared the street, he coached her. "Shift gently, the way you'd want a man to touch you. No jerking or tugging, just a slow, steady pressure."

Shelby moved her feet, depressing the clutch, shifting, then letting up on the pedal. His soft-spoken encouragement chased away her jitters. The transmission reacted like a dream.

Campus was just up the road. If she was going to divest herself of her passenger, it would have to be soon. Like, now.

When the car was up to speed, she gave it another

go.

The old college try, she thought.

"You have to get out of my car. Either you tell me where to drop you, or I'm going straight to campus security and let them help you out. Your choice."

"You're not going to believe me until you see for yourself what the situation is." He gave her a sad smile. Waved a hand between them. "Campus security. Let's just get this over with."

Chapter 6

Shelby didn't get out of the car when she pulled up to the wooden security kiosk. It was built like a London telephone booth, except the door remained wide open and it wasn't painted bright red. The silver nameplate on the guard's starched shirt did little to brighten his drab gray uniform.

He leaned out of the kiosk, clipboard in hand. As she'd driven up, she'd noticed he jotted her license plate number on the paper clipped to the board.

"Can't say I see too many shiny dream cars come past me." He gave an appreciative whistle and shook his head so hard his cap tilted. "Man, but she's a beauty."

Her window was down so she hung her elbow out and, resting the other hand oh-so casually on the steering wheel, gave him a megawatt smile. The guy's interest was on the car, so the smile was mostly ignored but that was fine by her. As long as he helped rid her of this Joey character, she didn't give a shit whether he even acknowledged her existence.

"Thanks. A birthday gift."

Another whistle. "You must really have him wrapped around your finger, little lady. No dude gives away a car like this unless he's over-the-moon in love with a chick."

She wished Turner felt that way. She'd gotten a

generic, lame card and promise of a "celebratory dinner" when it was more convenient. And that, she knew, meant burgers with the brothers or pizza after a rush party.

But her love life—or lack of one—wasn't the reason she idled near the guard's station.

"Look, I've got to get to class, but I need a favor."

He pulled his gaze from the sleek chassis and gave her a questioning look. Again, she smiled, and this time he gave her a grin in return. The guy couldn't be more than thirty, but already looked beaten down. A ring on his left hand told her he was married so she didn't bother ramping up the charm.

"What can I do for you?"

She opened her mouth to explain, but he cut her off with a wave of his Bic.

"I see you don't have a parking slip on your dash. I'll just write one up, and you'll be on your way." He ruffled the papers on his clipboard, pulled a pink parking pass from the bottom, and began to fill it in.

She hadn't realized she'd need a new pass. The old one was still in Betty, her dependable Dodge Dart that had so many miles on it her father deemed it unsafe. Wishing it was Betty's big wheel she gripped now, she ran through the possible ways to broach the subject with the guard when he'd finished with the paperwork.

No option seemed perfect. Having strangers booted from her vehicle was a new experience.

When he handed the pink rectangle through the window, she accepted it and dutifully put in on the dash where it could be seen from outside the car. Security patrols ticketed those without a pass, and a ticket was something she did not want.

"What else can I do you for?" The pen tapped the clipboard as he visually checked her tires.

"Um, Hank…I have a favor to ask."

He looked up when he heard his name. Good thinking, to check the name tag.

"Ask away. Want me to park this thing for you? Valet, at your service!" The joke gave her a reason to smile, so she did.

"No, thanks. I think I can handle that." She took a deep breath, then nodded to the passenger. "I hate to ask, but can you help this gentleman out of my car?"

Hank leaned down. He looked in the car, past her, at the passenger seat. A frown turned his features hard. When he met her gaze, friendliness had dissipated.

"I don't have time for jokes, kid." His tone was as hard as his scowl.

"I know you don't, and honestly, I wouldn't ask you to help me but this guy really won't leave and I don't know what to do." It came out in a rush. To her embarrassment, her throat tightened. Tears, something she hated, weren't far off. Gulping a breath, she waved to the figure beside her. "I have to get to class. I can't leave him in the car. My luck, he'd steal it, and my father would have my head if I let that happen. I've tried, but he won't go so please, just help him out."

Hank slapped his thigh with the clipboard. His gaze swept the interior of the car, the little that there was of it, anyhow, before resting on her face.

"I don't appreciate being the butt of these pranks. You may not believe it, but Campus Security is a vital part of university life. We do a big service for you, your parents, your professors, and every visitor who sets foot on this campus. What we don't need—and certainly don't appreciate—is having our valuable time taken up by spoiled brats like you who think it's a gas to harass us."

Crap. The guy had gone from friendly to ferocious in a heartbeat. And she still had Joey-what's-his-name in her car.

"I'm sorry—really, I am. I just thought you could get him out because I can't. He won't leave—no matter how many times I tell him to just get out."

Hank closed his eyes and tilted his head back. Had he not been aggravated he could have been grabbing some sun on his cheeks, but she knew better. She could almost hear the man counting to ten in his mind.

"He can't see me." Joey's voice was so calm and, since he made no effort to speak in an undertone, believable. As if reading her mind, he raised his voice and shouted, "Can you, Hanky Panky? You can't see or hear me, no matter how this gorgeous chickadee asks you to help her. You're just too damn stupid!"

Shelby gasped. It was bad enough the guard was already angry; now his intelligence was being loudly insulted. She turned, her mouth open and words of apology ready to tumble out, but Hank's head was still tilted back.

He hadn't heard a word.

She faced the figure beside her. "I-I…um, why, I mean what…oh, crap."

Hank leaned down and with a calmer tone said, "You need to go to class now. And if you know what's good for you, you won't come back to disturb the security force with silly pranks. Understood?"

All she managed was a silent nod before she got the car in gear and drove to the parking lot. It was almost full, but she found a spot at the far end, near the Fine Arts Building, and pulled in. Killed the engine.

And sat, for what felt like an hour but was only five minutes. Thoughts swirled in her head, so many she couldn't separate one from another.

Maybe she really had lost her mind. Not a passing thought, like the one she'd had in the orchard. But a hard point to ponder, finally snapping. After her mother's death, her aunt had worried she would have a grief-induced breakdown. Or get hooked on marijuana. Neither had happened—then. But now? Something was going on.

He sighed. "You're confused, Shelby." His tone was gentle again, and she was grateful he didn't call her babe or sweetie or any other endearment. A minute passed before he broke the silence again. "I've had a long time to come to grips with this, but it's all new to you. I know you're upset, and I'm sure you're scared, but I promise I'm not here to hurt you."

Her hands were still on the steering wheel so she unwrapped her fingers from the death grip and put them in her lap. They shook, but not as badly as they had when she'd first seen him.

She looked over. Met his gaze. If she had to guess, she'd say he was sincere.

Telling the truth.

Holy shit, he was telling the truth. It hit her like a blast of ice water.

She wasn't crazy.

"You're a ghost." It came upon a breath, so quiet it was barely a whisper.

"That's what I've been trying to tell you."

Chapter 7

Joey watched her walk across the parking lot. She never turned back, not even when she reached the wide, paved walkway that wound past trees, benches and brick buildings. It was as if she was determined to put the car—and him—completely behind her.

Out of sight, out of mind.

Not that he could blame her one bit for wanting to be away from him. It was written right on that pretty face of hers how she felt about being in close company with someone like him. No, that wasn't right. Some*thing* like him. When a guy goes from living to dead, he exchanges the *one* for *thing*. Like it or not— and he most definitely did not.

Hell's bells. His life had been complicated enough, but this whole post-life gig was even worse. When he was alive, he wasn't trapped to a material object. He could touch a woman, hold her close, and feel her breath on his cheek. Sitting next to Shelby, he'd been acutely aware that all those options were closed to him. Forever.

Sorrow slammed him. Hard. When he'd been newly dead, he'd had moments of self-pity, bouts of sadness for all he'd lost. The opportunities he'd believed he had endless time to turn from dream to reality. He'd mourned for the loss of his life—but it had been a fleeting circumstance.

He only had a vague idea of how to get himself out of this between-world limbo. It had something to do with Shelby, the woman, and the Shelby Cobra. How the two were linked was still unclear, but maybe if he paid attention, the task would show itself. It had to be some kind of trial, a feat of either strength or morals that he had to accomplish in order to gain access to heaven.

If he didn't complete the test, it was very possible he'd spend eternity with a pitchfork in his hand, shoveling coal for Old Scratch himself.

"I'd better figure out how to save the day for Shelby," he muttered. She was long gone, lost to the college crowd. "That's the rub, the whole reason I'm stuck riding shotgun in my own car. I've got to save another's soul to save my own." He tilted his head back, the way the guard had. The sun didn't warm him, but he remembered how it was supposed to feel so imagined his skin kissed by its rays. "So Saint Peter, if that's what it takes to waltz up to your Pearly Gates, that's what I'll do. But hell, could you give a guy a sign? Show me what I'm supposed to save the damsel from? She sure as shit doesn't look like she's in any distress to me—unless you count being spooked by a ghost, that is."

Must be he was fated to figure the particulars out on his own, because neither the Pearly Gatekeeper nor any of his subordinates made a showing to point him in the right direction. He looked around the car, even behind it, before giving up on the messenger.

Why should the afterlife be any less bumpy than his life had been? He must've been nuts to even hope it would be.

Damn. Why had he died with such a cherry of a car at such a young age? He couldn't have bought the farm as an old geezer, instead? The whole bit about life not being fair was only the tip of the iceberg. Life after life was even less fair—but who would know that before they reached this point and it happened to them?

Loud male voices caught his attention.

Four young men sauntered his way. They didn't see him, of course.

All wore Greek letters on their blue long-sleeve jerseys. Each had the look of being from the right side of town, something he recognized because he had never been from the moneyed side. Always the outsider looking in, he knew without being told none of these guys had empty wallets, or hollow bellies.

"Turner, you going out with Heather again tonight?" The boy who asked poked the shoulder of the handsomest of the bunch. He was pushed off, amid howls of laughter.

"I bet he is." The second one waved a hand in the air, as if cooling his face. "Hot Heather, a guy's best friend."

The one who was being teased grinned. He looked as if he owned the world and held it all right in the palm of his hand.

Joey hated him immediately. It was unfounded and illogical but hell, that didn't matter at all, now did it? He was dead and perfectly within his rights to like—or, in this case, despise—anyone he chose.

He clenched a fist. Had he been alive, and able to feel the touch of skin on skin, he would've loved to give the guy a jab, just for the hell of it.

"Hey, a guy's gotta get his kicks somewhere,

doesn't he?" Mr. Slick Frat Boy smoothed his hair back, the action so perfect Joey would've put money on it that the jerk practiced in front of a mirror. "Can't blame me for wanting to get a piece of what she's giving away."

The last guy, the only one with a pock-marked face and arms too long for his body, shook his head. It earned him a poke from the first guy—which he pushed away.

"I don't know." The gangly one took a wide step from his friends, putting a foot or so between himself and the finger poker. "If I had someone as pretty as Shelby, I don't think I'd be wasting my time with Heather. Any guy can get Heather, but Shelby? She's another story."

The gigolo snorted. "I've already got Shelby. There's no harm in having a squeeze on the side. I mean, you wouldn't want me to wear my girl down to the bone, would you?" He shrugged, the bravado making the gesture larger than life. "I've got man-sized needs, I tell you. And that little lady? Let's just say she's too delicate for the kind of action I've got in mind."

Finger Poker put a hand over his eyes, as if it was all too much for his sensitive nature to bear. But as they turned and headed toward the far end of the parking lot, he said, "We've all heard about your so-called needs, Stud Walker. If I were you, I'd be careful—even Heather can be broken. The girl you side-dated last semester ended up in the hospital, remember? Shit, if Shelby ever found out about that—"

"She's not gonna find out, because none of you are going to say a thing. We're brothers, right? What happens between brothers stays between brothers."

The gangly one stuck his neck out a bit. "Even brotherhood has its limits."

It was a good thing Joey didn't need oxygen any longer because he'd been holding his breath for several minutes. It was impossible to breathe through the rage coursing through him.

Turner Walker.

The vermin boyfriend who didn't deserve a girl like Shelby Carmichael.

That had to be his mission. Save the girl from the rat—and head off to heaven.

It would be a simple task if he were allowed to just kill the bastard, but he was pretty sure murder wasn't one of the options open to the dead-vying-for-admittance-to-the-clouds crowd.

Chapter 8

Lit 210: Hemingway, a Perspective was one of Shelby's elective courses. One that she actually enjoyed, just for the sheer love of the prolific author's words. Tucked in with her mandatory curriculum, the three hours each week were bright spots in the Freudian-Jungian-psychoanalytical jungle that she'd chosen for her major.

Her mother had majored in literature, and she would have followed in those footsteps, but her father deemed it too frivolous. His daughter should study more serious academia, something worth the time, effort, and money they were investing in her schooling. He'd suggested sociology, but she didn't have the stomach for dealing with serious issues that plagued society's downtrodden, so she opted for psychology. Better to unravel the psyche than anything more pressing.

Minoring in literature put extra demands on her, class and grade-wise, but it was worth it.

Professor McMann, a roundish, white-haired, red-cheeked man who looked more like Kris Kringle than an expert on the written word, paced the front of the lecture hall. Every step he punctuated with a tap of the walking stick that was never out of his hand. Gossipers insisted the man slept with the carved maple stick, but that was pure speculation, since the professor was a lifelong bachelor who insisted Keats, Chaucer, and Longfellow were stimulating enough bedfellows.

And, of course, Papa Hemingway.

She didn't need to take notes. She'd already read—and re-read—the book being discussed, so she sat back and listened to the lecture.

"We all know Hemingway relied on themes to convey his message in his work. Love. War. Loss. He goes outside the box with regard to location, setting his tales in distant lands. Paris. Spain. Africa. What does this tell us—the way he places his themes in spots which most of his readers—remember the time frame when his work was first published—would never have the opportunity to see?"

Turner was also in the class. He and one fraternity brother, Gil Howland, sat in the very last row. Shelby knew he expected her and Gil to carry him through the course. She'd helped him with an essay but let his brother do the rest. If he couldn't sit with her and Tania, one of the Omicron Kappas, he could damn well do his own coursework.

Being cozy outside of school, when he was either drunk or stoned and they were at a party, was less significant than sitting in class with her. One was typical frat boy behavior; the other a full-on public show of attachment.

It riled her that he chose to appear unattached in front of everyone. When he had her alone, he made it clear that he desired to be very attached to her. In a very private way.

Down in the front, a girl answered. Shelby hadn't been listening to her reply, but it must have been adequate because the professor continued.

"That's right. Hemingway put his quite ordinary themes into extraordinary settings. By doing so, he made the point that man's suffering, as well as his joy, is universal. Life, death, rebirth…basic human conditions applicable to one and all."

A snort from behind them. No need to turn to see who the disrespectful student was—her boyfriend never had an issue with making his opinion known, often in a derogatory manner.

Tania elbowed her when she sighed. A folded slip of paper dropped onto her open book when the other woman passed her hand through the air. As unobtrusively as possible, Shelby unfolded the note.

Why do you put up with that guy?

Why, indeed? She asked herself that question almost as often as her sorority sisters did. She still hadn't found an answer that satisfied any of them.

Taking her pen, she scribbled, *I don't know*, and passed the note back.

Professor McMann had turned his lecture to the book they were currently working on.

"In *The Sun Also Rises* Hemingway embraces two major themes. The wounded soldier, in love with the heroine but unable to perform, his masculinity lost in the struggle for freedom, clearly is almost a poster boy for the emasculated hero. He wants, yearns, even, yet is unable to get what—or who—he desires in the manner any man would consider optimal. Any questions?"

Again, a snort from the back. Turner must've commented, as well, because a low titter from those nearest him cut the silence. If the professor noticed, he ignored the rude behavior.

"Secondly, this novel explores the role of women

in society. This heroine is complex; she evokes sympathy, yet she's not afraid to go after what she wants. Promiscuous, but willing to remain in a relationship that cannot satisfy her needs. She gives too much of herself, without thinking about what—or who—she really is. What she needs. What she actually, in her heart of hearts, wants."

"I'll give her what she needs." The lewd comment carried.

This time the scholar called his student on it. "Mr. Walker? Do you have something to add to the lecture? Because I'm always open to an intellectually-stimulating comment."

The room was silent, except for the shuffling feet Shelby was certain belonged to one big-mouthed fraternity brother.

She was mortified when the professor dropped his gaze from surveying Turner to meet hers. The unspoken question, whatever was she doing with such a jerk, hung between them. Heat rose from her neck to her cheeks.

Professor McMann tapped his stick hard against the tile. "As I thought; nothing intellectual to add. Let's continue…" He looked up, scrutinizing the drop lighting hanging from the high ceiling in the large hall for a long moment. "Hemingway is ultimately giving one of his most profound commentaries on the dynamics between the sexes."

She shot a quick glance at the big wall clock. Class was nearly over, thank goodness.

Tania reached over and patted her hand.

The professor sent his point home. "The relationship between these two is doomed from the start. It is not viable, can never end happily and, despite the woman's willingness to settle for less than she deserves, is a catastrophe in the making."

The last words, declared as the bell pealed, were delivered with a serious expression on the teacher's face—his gaze locked on Shelby. Her mouth went dry because she had no misconceptions about the man's message.

Catastrophe.

The word rang in her head as she stood and dashed for the closest exit.

Chapter 9

Omicron Kappa Pi alumna owned the big, periwinkle-blue Victorian house with white gingerbread trim on Cherry Street. It was a mint location, right at the intersection so the spacious, wraparound porch faced two streets which meant better vantage points for watching who came and went from nearby houses. The yard wasn't too large, but the wide walkway leading up to the steps was perfect for song lines and impromptu sister gatherings.

The active sisters were fortunate to have housing that offered fairly inexpensive private rooms per semester, was clean, well-maintained, and secure. Those assets didn't apply to all off-campus housing, but the alumna took care of their own.

The rage of raids and panty runs put all sororities on high alert, ever mindful of the inebriated antics of the nearby frat houses. It was good to know their panties were reasonably safe.

More than anything, Shelby longed to live in the house, but it wouldn't have been fair to ditch her father. Their home was large, and even with both of them there was room to spare. She could imagine how awful he'd feel if he were left alone to rattle around in the beautiful rooms on his own.

She wanted to move out. But obligation kept her from broaching the subject.

Terrible to be the only child, with no one to share the joys of childhood or responsibilities of adulthood. She'd hoped for siblings when she was little, but they never came, no matter how hard she prayed or how often she'd asked.

Omicron Kappa more than made up for her lack of natural siblings. They were the sisters she'd craved, and she appreciated every one of them.

Even the quirky ones. Like Kaylee Jackson, who spent most of her free time driving to head-banger rock shows. She was notoriously persuasive, and usually could wheedle, cajole, or bribe another sister to accompany her on a road trip. But she was a true free spirit and not afraid to venture off on her own.

The walls of Kaylee's room were covered with rock music posters. On every inch of all available space, popular (and not-so-popular) groups strutted in various poses. It made for interesting decoration and hid the puke green paint the room's previous sister had left behind.

Twin beds, set against opposite walls in the compact space, along with an enormous white leather bean bag chair provided room to sprawl. Now, Kaylee laid across her bed, her stockinged feet on her pillows, while Tania sat on the other bed and polished her toenails.

Shelby loved the bean bag and didn't mind being close to the floor. She stretched her legs, put her feet on the bed beside Tania, and folded her hands.

They'd fled campus for the house after the lit class, knowing Kaylee's schedule was clear for the afternoon. She was already acing her psych course so blowing off one lecture was no big deal.

The embarrassment of being Turner's girlfriend had been discussed—in detail—already, with the horror in Hemingway analyzed so thoroughly Shelby was nauseated.

As any sister knew, the cure for male-induced nausea was soda and chips. In copious amounts.

They each had a bag of chips and soda bottles by their sides.

"I just don't get why you let him treat you like that." Tania stuck her left leg out straight and gave a critical look at her painted toenails. She had already done the other foot so now she hung her legs off the edge of the bed so they could dry. "He's a jerk—and makes no attempt to hide it. Come on, Shel, you could have any guy on campus. Drop this clown, already."

"I get it, I really do, but it's easy for you to give advice when you've got a dream like Chad."

Chad Urbansky was not a fraternity brother. He was almost a complete opposite of the frat boys they spent so much time with. Tania's beau was head of the debate team, leader of the national scholastic organization, and had a 3.8 GPA. To top it off, he did modeling for magazines when he could squeeze in photo shoots. He was the jackpot, boyfriend-wise, and they all knew it.

Tania already wore a pre-engagement ring. It was the most perfectly-brilliant sapphire surrounded by tiny diamonds, and every time she waved her hand the other girls practically drooled. No one begrudged her the good match, but they all wished they'd be as lucky and find their own Chad.

Turner was nowhere near Chad in the boyfriend department. Who was she trying to kid? He wasn't even on the same planet as Tania's hunk.

"I know, but you can do so much better. Can't she, Kaylee?"

"Of course she can. But you and I—and every other sister—can say that until our eyes pop out of our heads. It's not going to change anything until sweet sister here decides for herself she's sick and tired of being that asshole's door mat." She took a long pull of her soda, gave a rather unladylike burp, and nodded toward the closet. "Anyone care for a shot of rum in theirs? Give this party a little pop?"

Both women shook their heads.

The sapphire ring breezed through the air. "I'm going to dinner with Chad. Then to the library—he's helping with my statistics homework. Ugh."

Kaylee waved an admonishing finger. "You shouldn't take classes like that, with all those numbers. I'm sure Chad's going to take care of you financially; you'll never need to bother balancing a checkbook and you definitely won't have any use for those idiotic statistical rules."

The sisters came from all over the country. It was interesting to see that their points of origin influenced their ideas on women's rights, marriage, and equality. Bra burning hadn't been in the news for a few years, replaced by the oil shortage and recession, but sometimes it was as if no Playtex Cross-Your-Heart had even been scorched.

Kaylee's southern accent matched her Georgia peach opinion on gender roles.

Shelby shared an eye roll with Tania.

"Look, Tania is smart enough to balance her own checkbook. And the statistics might come in handy if she ever decides to get a job where that's, I don't know, something she needs to know. But the point is, she shouldn't have to rely on a man to give her a solid future."

Kaylee gave a southern-belle pout, the kind that got her teased by the girls and chased by the guys. She had showed them all a photo album of her cotillion, where she'd worn a white gown covered in ruffles. Beneath the frou-frou flounces, her whole damsel-in-distress persona covered a steely determination.

"I agree. But that doesn't mean a gal can't let a man keep her in baubles and bells. While she, of course, stashes her own mad money on the side." The grin made it all seem less mercenary.

"Right, but I still think a woman should be able to take care of herself." Her mother had relied on her husband for every nickel. Not that he ever begrudged her a penny, but it was the idea that the only money she had was what he gave her. Shelby didn't want that kind of reliance in her own marriage.

Independence. It couldn't be more paramount to a woman's well-being, both physically and emotionally.

"Listen, we're all on the same page." Kaylee finished her soda, set the bottle on the floor beside her bed, and lifted one groomed brow. "But I've got to ask—who paid for that sexy little roadster? Hmm?"

"We know it wasn't Mr. Frat Loser." Tania winked, softening the nickname with a smile. "Did your dad give it to you?"

So much for advocating for women's rights and independence. The spiel went down the proverbial drain in a quick swish.

"Yeah, for my birthday."

Tania touched up her big toe, then twisted the Cover Girl bottle closed. She dropped it into the open pocket on her backpack. It lay on the floor beside the bed, with her Frye boots beside it. "You could sound a little more grateful, chickie."

Shelby sighed. "I don't like the car."

Kaylee snorted—something she certainly did not learn at her mama's knee. "Why the hell not? That car is a peach!"

"My father pinned the stupid car name on me, and that's bad enough. But now, to have to drive around in one? Not my idea of perfect, let me tell you."

The other two exchanged glances.

"I'll trade you my beat-up Pinto for the Shelby. Just let me get the keys for you." Tania leaned down, rummaged in her bag, and took out the key ring.

"Tell you what—you can have the car. Just give me Chad, and we'll call it done." She teased, knowing no car—or yacht, or house, or anything else—could part the pair.

"Sister, there aren't enough men like Chad in heaven or on earth that could make me foolish enough to give him away."

Chapter 10

Twilight claimed day. Then, darkness fell.

Light pooled on the wide front porch of the old Victorian, spilling from unshuttered windows. Laughter, soft and lilting, carried on the breeze. He had no idea exactly how many young women were in the house, but from his position on the hood of the Shelby, it sounded like dozens. Occasionally, hundreds.

Times changed, but women apparently didn't. Thriving without men, stronger than they knew, and changing the world one inch at a time, they were the backbone of the species. Twenty years ago, they'd been keeping the country alive after world wars begun by men. Now, they seemed sturdier, even. Wearing pants and running rings around jerks like that Walker guy.

He'd always appreciated an independent woman.

Joey ran a hand through his hair. Long ago he'd lost the amazement at being, even post mortem, physically intact. Initially he worried he'd degrade, but nothing had changed. His hair felt as it had in life.

"Hey, amigo." The voice was tequila smooth, with an accent that gave its Mexican origin away. "How's it hanging?" Alfonso drew out the last syllable as he leaned against a maple tree that grew on the strip of grass separating sidewalk from pavement. An unlit hand-rolled cigarette dangled from his fingers.

Alfonso was the first of his own kind he'd met.

Another dead guy, stuck between earth and heaven—or hell, depending on which way the wind blew.

The other ghost didn't have any answers about their state, either, but at least his presence made the whole mess less lonely.

"Hanging to the left, man. Always, to the left." The little joke made them both grin. They never began a conversation without the nod to Alfonso's first greeting all those years ago.

His friend never shared what his actual life had been like, but Joey suspected it hadn't been easy. Patched, faded jeans, a frayed denim button-down shirt and scuffed work boots pretty much gave away his station in life. The only bit of color was the striped belt holding baggy pants on slim hips. One time, long ago, he'd commented that his wife had woven the belt.

His friend wasn't nearly as anxious to move past heaven's gates as Joey, but the reason for his reluctance was, as were so many other details, something he kept to himself. Joey never pressed.

Hard enough being dead. Being dead with the fifty-question treatment? Who needed that?

"Status quo, then. Good, that's good… So, *que pasa*?" He pointed to the house with the cigarette. "Never would've pegged you for a Peeping Tom."

"I'm not peeping."

A slow look between the car and the house, then a low chuckle. "Where I come from, any amigo sitting in the dark outside a houseful of ladies, looking in the windows, would get a serious ass-kicking. Usually from a pretty chica's padre. Or her big brothers. That place sounds like Chica Central, man. Gotta be a lot of daddies willing to open a can of whoop ass if they see you skulking."

"I'm not skulking." He crossed his arms over his chest. "And in case you've forgotten, no one can see us so even if we go over there and press our noses against the glass, we're home free."

"Ah, yes. The little fact of our curious existence." Alfonso stuck the cigarette between his lips. Crossed his arms, too. Then, he nodded. "Too bad those three aren't dead. Anyone sees them, there's gonna be some serious hell to pay."

Chapter 11

Walker led the others across the lawn. They crouched, chins nearly touching knees as they ran between garage and shrubbery. Beneath a bay window, they pushed the branches of a wide rhododendron aside and pressed into the space beside the house.

"*Tres culebras*." Alfonso stuck out his hand and wiggled his index finger in the air. "Three snakes, slithering up to do no good. Years pass, but the snake is as old as the Garden of Eden, eh?"

"Some things will never change." He shot a thumb toward the house. "What do you say? Feel like beating the bushes?"

A shrug. "Hell, yes. It's not like I've got anything else to do."

No need to crouch or hide, so they walked across the lawn. The moon, rising behind them, did not cast their shadows on the grass. Joey noticed, then dismissed, the phenomenon. He kept his gaze on the whispering fools hiding in the foliage.

They stopped on the lawn side of the bush. The trio was within arms' reach. And, within earshot, despite their low tones.

Walker rose slowly, his eyes just clearing the lower windowsill. He swiveled his head, looking from side to side. His two companions remained in squatting positions. The reek of rum wafted up when one whispered something that made the other snicker.

"Shh!" Their leader swatted the space behind him, catching one guy on the side of the head. The slap was louder than their words. "Shut the hell up, you two."

Joey and Alfonso peeked into the room. The sight was a single guy's dream come true.

Pretty young women, everywhere. Slouched in overstuffed armchairs. Crowded onto two extra-long beige sofas. Sitting cross-legged on the floor. Laughing, talking, and eating pizza.

Alfonso put a hand over his eyes. "Save me from myself! I don't know if it's the pizza or the señoritas, but my mouth is watering."

"Mine, too." It took only a second to spot Shelby. In a roomful of women, she stood right out, sparkling like the brightest star in the night sky. His breath caught when he saw her perched on the edge of a low ottoman. She shared it with another girl, but he only had eyes for her.

The slices could be the greatest on the planet, but what attracted him definitely didn't come from a pizza oven.

Walker motioned the others to stand. They did— and stared into the house as if they'd never seen women before.

"Put your eyes back in your heads." Walker pointed to Shelby. "Especially that one—keep your damn eyes off her. She's all mine."

"Arrogant, isn't he?" Alfonso took a step closer.

Joey's fists clenched at his sides. "You have no idea."

"Back in the day, we saw a lot of snakes in the mountains. Above Vera Cruz, mostly, but some down in the villages." A hard expression matched Alfonso's biting words. "When we marched with Hidalgo, we took care of hundreds of snakes like these. Some, the two-legged kind but a lot of slithery ones, too. You get my drift?"

He'd never asked, but through the years Joey pieced together the sobering fact that Alfonso died over two hundred years ago. The Mexican War of Independence, and Hidalgo's revolt, took place in 1810.

And Alfonso was there. Revolting. Fighting. Killing snakes.

He pushed the thought aside. "I get it, all right."

Walker pointed as he spoke. "See the front door? When the meeting's over, they'll all leave that way. But that other door leads to the back porch. Just past the door is a back stairway. Go up to the bedrooms on the second floor and snag some panties."

One guy shook his head. "I don't know. How the hell are we supposed to do that without detection?"

"Just do it, Candy Ass. If you want to be a brother, you'll have to get used to sliding in and out of sorority houses without being seen." Walker smacked a fist against his chest. "Me? I'm like Tarzan, swinging from bed to bed without even getting my pants wrinkled."

Joey's hand shot out. He shoved the braggart forward so hard Walker's forehead almost collided with the window frame.

Alfonso whistled. "Nice reflexes, amigo."

"Hey! What the hell?" Walker looked behind him. The others did, too. Of course, there was nothing to see except the bare branches of the rhododendron.

"You tripped." The mostly silent guy slurred his words. "I saw it, you tripped. Must be the booze."

"It's not the booze. One of you assholes pushed me."

The other guy shook his head. "Wasn't me. Musta been the other asshole."

"Was not." He pointed to the window. "I still don't think we can get any panties."

Walker snorted. "Take them off the girls if you have to, but don't come out here without at least one pair apiece. And make sure they've been worn—I'll be sniffing them to see—"

This time, Walker sustained a push so hard he bounced off the guy beside him.

"*Cabrón*," Alfonso muttered.

Joey knew enough Spanish to recognize *asshole* when he heard it.

The three weren't so drunk that they didn't realize something was going on. They turned, one to the other, with wide eyes and accusations flying from their lips.

Walker was angry enough that his voice rose. "Listen, you shit, you don't touch a brother!"

"I didn't—he musta done it."

"Did not!"

When the third one spoke, Joey slapped the first accomplice on the back of the head.

"Shit! What the hell did you do that for?" Drunkenness clouded his judgment. He slapped Walker on the shoulder. "You don't have to touch me. I'm not a pledge yet—and even if I were, you don't have to freaking hit me, man."

"What the—hell, you'll never be a brother now! You shouldn't have put your grimy paw on me, jerk." Walker pulled his arm back to hit the guy, but before he could follow through, Joey pushed the other drunk into him.

The three stumbled, a tangle of arms and legs, against the house.

Thud. Slaps. Shoves. A few punches erupted. *Thud. Thump.*

They crashed through the branches and onto the lawn. A three-man drunken scuffle, so fast and furious it was almost impossible to tell who was taking the worst of it.

Alfonso and Joey grinned at each other when faces appeared at the glass. The window flew up.

"Hey—what's going on out there?" The indignant voice cut the night air.

Then, a chorus of female voices.

"I'm calling the cops!"

"Probably those damn frat jerks again, after our panties!"

The front door opened, and a parade of beautiful women ran onto the porch. Some still held slices of pizza. Others, cans of diet soda. One had a big wooden paddle over her shoulder.

Walker broke free from the skirmish and ran for the edge of the property.

"Not so fast, asshole." Joey was swifter in death than in life. He stuck his foot out.

Walker tripped—then flew. His face met the ground, and when he swore, he got a mouthful of grass. He pushed himself to his knees, but the temptation was too great. It might not get him to heaven any sooner, but Joey didn't care; he planted a knee on Walker's back and sent him back down onto the ground.

Alfonso clapped. "That's the way—keep the snake in the grass!"

Chapter 12

Dinner at the sorority house—pizza delivery for twenty-four sisters—took a while. They were interrupted by the scuffle outside, which, although entertaining, gave them an extra delay.

The Pineapple Punch Meet and Greet Rush party took place before dinner, so they got a late start. It was the last rush event of the semester, and no one wanted to cut it short.

Chapter meeting afterward took an additional hour.

Discussing potential candidates was a thoughtful process. Not every girl who rushed a sorority was given a bid, so the personalities as well as the potential for growth in the sisterhood had to be brought to the table. At this point, there were a dozen potentials, so the discussion was long—and sometimes lively.

By the time Shelby opened the car door and got in, she was bone tired.

And not in the mood to argue with a ghost. She didn't know exactly when she realized that the vehicle visitor was a real live, honest-to-goodness envoy from the hereafter, only that she did.

So why was he here?

Like it or not, she was stuck with him. He smiled at her from the passenger seat when she tossed her stuff on the floor near his boots.

Tired blew off a tad when faced with the dimples

his smile produced. His cheeks were lightly stubbled. Five o'clock shadow had an alarming—and instant— effect on her girl parts.

Which totally defied the weariness she thought would consume her only a few minutes before.

"Welcome back." Another grin, and a second wave of heat to the apex of her thighs.

"Have you been here the whole time?"

"Yep."

She pushed the key into the slot but did not turn it. "Can't you leave? Get away from the car?"

He sighed.

A circle of light from the streetlamp touched the nose of the car and brought a glow to its interior. It was enough to see his dimples and smile, but did not brighten things well enough to see into his eyes.

The sigh made up for that. She didn't need to witness his expression to know longing or resignation when she heard it.

"I can, but it's not easy. I mean, it's not hard to do, but it drains my energy."

"How much energy do you have?"

"I don't know. I've never tested myself to the end of my endurance." A silence. Then, "I haven't had any reason to do that. Since my demise, things have been pretty tame. Quiet. Dull as dirt, actually."

With her mother's passing, Shelby had contemplated the hereafter a time or two. Or more. But only in the broadest terms. She'd wondered about her mother's peacefulness now that her mortal suffering was ended. She'd prayed her mother could see her— especially all her accomplishments, as if she were still sharing them.

Never had she thought the afterlife might be dull.

"What do you do? In heaven, I mean?"

Another sigh. Longer than the first.

"Well… I haven't actually made it there."

She lifted an eyebrow. "So, you're from hell?"

His hand cut the air between them, a fast wave that brought a cool current near her face.

"No! Of course not."

"Well, if you're not from heaven, it makes sense that you're from hell, doesn't it?"

Shelby hadn't been much of a church-goer since her mother's illness. Before the ALS, theirs was one of the no-miss families at St. Matthew's Catholic Church. Week after week, third row, center. She'd made her communion and confirmation, and her parents expected her to take her wedding vows before the same altar where her mother's casket rested during the funeral service.

That was the last time she'd set foot in the church.

It was a combination of things that kept her from St. Matthew's these days. Partly the memories of that awful final experience—the music her mother loved so much, overpowering aroma of roses from the many floral arrangements and myriad of other things that were designed to comfort the grieving but which cut her heart open even more. She'd tried to block so much from her mind; staying out of church kept any of it from creeping back in.

Also, the Word had been shoved down her throat her whole life, but when crunch time came, her knock had not been answered.

Yeah, she was plenty pissed at the Higher Power.

But wiping a lifetime of catechism classes off her

heart and out of her mind was impossible. The ghost wasn't from heaven? Then he had to be one of the red suit, pitchfork-carrying ones. It was the only other choice.

The semi-darkness in the car felt as concealing as the confessional.

"Nothing makes sense anymore, babe."

She let it pass; maybe if he confessed to being from hell she could take him to church and throw holy water on him. Or something. But better to let the *babe* bit ride. There were bigger issues to hammer out.

"I don't understand." She left the key in the ignition and put her hands on her lap. Folded—as if in prayer, a totally subconscious act if ever there was one. For a second she contemplated untwining her fingers, conscious of what Freud would say of the posture, but it was comfortable so she stayed as she was.

"Me, either. I've had a long time to think about everything, and I still don't understand. Maybe I never will."

"Well, if you're not from heaven and you're not from hell, where are you from?"

Again, he sighed. A chill inside the car made her nipples come to attention.

"I'm from Port Trane, the podunk dairy town where your father found the car. I'm from there, even though I swear I'd never been in that barn before the car was towed there the day after I died."

"Was your body still in the car? Is that what happened?" It was a disgusting thought, his dead—possibly rotting—corpse in the car for a length of time. Relief flooded her when he shook his head. "Well then, what the hell happened?"

A low tolerance for guessing games mixed with frustration.

"Well, you don't mince words, do you?"

"I'm tired," she admitted. She yawned behind her hand. "Sorry."

"Don't apologize. Hey, it's been a long day for you. Why don't we head home? We can take this up in the morning."

Shelby blinked, wondering what her father would say when he saw the occupant of the prized automobile. As if he read her mind, her passenger chuckled.

"No, I won't be going inside your house with you. And no, your father won't see me. This is between us, Shelby—just you and me. And the Cobra."

Too exhausted to attempt to unravel the mystery that had suddenly become her life, she started the car and headed for home.

Chapter 13

Joey had spent the endless nighttime hours sitting on the hood of the car. Looking up at the moon. Listening to crickets and watching fireflies. Hell, even bugs were busier, going about their normal lives while he imitated a bump on a log and watched the minutes creep past.

If there had been some kind of guidance—an envoy of the dead, maybe—to turn to, he would have gladly turned. In life, he'd been a complete loner, a do-it-himself-or-bust kind of guy who never, ever asked for help from anyone. That changed when he became dead. But now there was no one to appeal to for assistance.

Finally absolutely on his own...and yearning for a mentor.

Alfonso was his only dead friend, and he seemed to know even less about what was going on. Worse, it didn't bother him a bit being in limbo for two centuries.

Karma is a bitch, he thought as he watched the neighborhood come to life.

Next door, a guy in a ratty t-shirt stumbled out of a dented pop-up camper. A beer can rolled down the folding steps behind him as he made a beeline for the big maple on his side of the fence, unzipped, and did his business. Halfway through his morning whiz, he must've realized the evidence of his prior evening's adventure was in the grass. He barely zipped up before dashing for the empty Budweiser and crushing it in his hand.

The *One Day At A Time* slogan emblazoned across the guy's chest was for show. Death had given Joey perception he'd never had when alive, the ability to see beneath the façade most people presented to the world. The levels of character were deeper on some than on others; this neighbor was a liar about taking the sober path, and there wasn't any real need to dig to perceive that fact.

But the lie on the shirt hid something bigger.

He felt it. And a familiarity. The neighbor wasn't a stranger…

He dismissed the alcoholic from his mind when he sensed wakefulness inside the Carmichael residence. The ability to venture in and watch exactly what was going on was an option, but decency kept him from invading humans that way. Instead, he felt their movements—from a distance.

Along with enhanced discernment, he was gifted with other psychic abilities. And a few interesting tricks that came with having lost his physical body, which were weird at first, but he'd gotten used to them rather quickly. If he were the spying type, moving through solid objects—like walls—would be an asset.

Emotional reading was less entertaining than wall gliding. The emotions pulsing from the house, now that its occupants no longer slumbered, were intense. So many dark feelings that his own heart hurt.

Grief, sadness, regret—how could two people survive in that environment? He would have drowned in the place had he been alive. The weight of their combined sorrow was enough to suck the soul from anyone.

There was very little conversation before Shelby's father emerged. He took the front path with intensity. When he stopped beside the Cobra, some of the heaviness lifted from his step. He ran a loving hand down the bullet body, one fingertip tracing a heart against the metal. Then, his life settled again on his shoulders, and he crossed the yard to his car.

The thought that no man should drive a dark blue sedan—not unless he was an undercover cop—sped through Joey's head.

Shelby came out of the house a few minutes after her father.

His heart—or the place his heart used to beat— heated. A nice, comfortable warmth filled him. It had been so long since he experienced anything like it, it took a moment to recognize the all-too-human act.

Just as he allowed himself to pretend he was alive—if only for a few, self-indulgent moments—the world shifted. Intensified, as Shelby drew closer to the car.

Her aura was unique. The moment she woke, he felt her. Every emotion shifted her aural projection. He was acutely aware of her—all the time, an awareness that was like no other he felt for any being beside her.

Today she wore a white, open-collar t-shirt dress with the Omicron Kappa Pi insignia embroidered in blue across her left breast. The fabric was clingy and showed every curve. Bare legs and clear Jellies sandals made the look even more casual. Her hair was loose, hanging down past her shoulders in waves.

The memory of how it felt to run his fingers

through a woman's hair hit in a burst of clarity. Most of what he'd lost he tolerated without too much trouble, but some things about being alive he missed with a vengeance. Women, and how they felt, tore a hole in him whenever he let himself remember.

The black Impala rumbled as it stopped, idling at the end of the driveway. Shelby ran toward the car, her dress hugging her thighs. She nearly tripped when she caught a pebble beneath her right foot. The fall would have been nasty, but she caught herself just as the driver called.

"Hurry—I don't have all day."

Turner Walker, the biggest creep on campus.

Joey's fingers tightened into fists. The jerk didn't even have the decency to get out of the car and open the passenger door for her.

She tugged the door open, slid into the seat, and said, "I'm sorry. I didn't realize you have a nine o'clock class."

Walker reached across, his arm brushing her breasts, and pulled the door closed.

"I don't. I told the guys I'd hang out on the wall this morning." He ran a hand over his hair before pulling out onto the street. "I don't want to keep the brothers waiting. You know how it is."

Chapter 14

"For the love of God, why do you have to be so damn stubborn?" Turner smacked the steering wheel with the palm of one hand while the other slid inside his blazer. He pulled out a pack of Marlboros. Flipping the top back, he jiggled one cigarette out, grabbed it with his lips, and dropped the pack onto the seat between his thighs. His hand went back into the inner pocket.

"Watch the road. Turner—you're all over the place."

He narrowly avoided taking out a mailbox at the end of a driveway when he flicked the blue plastic Bic lighter he'd been carrying with the cigs and lit the Marlboro.

He exhaled, smiling around the smoke stream. "Wrapped too tight. That's your problem, you know. Just wrapped way too tight."

She rolled down the window on her door. He knew she hated smoking. He did it just to annoy her.

He could be such an asshole when he didn't get his way. Like now.

"I don't have a problem." Unless I count you, she thought. "And I'm not being stubborn. I'm just saying that I'm not going all the way to the city just to see some punk rock band. They're called the Disco Rats, and you want to drive hours to hear them? Sometimes I think you don't have an ounce of sense."

He turned and blew smoke her way. The glint in his eyes was hard. Angry. Definitely not the expression he shared with their friends, or her father. Or his, for that matter. No, this nasty glare was hers, and hers alone.

Sometimes she wondered who was the bigger idiot for staying in the relationship—Turner? Or her?

They were together longer than they would have been if they weren't both Greek. She'd made excuses and put up with his bad temper, bullying, and emotional abuse simply to keep conflict from forming between the Omicron Kappas and his brothers. Those things, the hard feelings left behind after an inter-Greek breakup, took a long time to heal. Shelby had never wanted to bring that to the sisters.

She wondered how much longer she could pretend things were okay for the sake of Greek relations.

"You're stubborn, and you don't have a sense of adventure. Any other chick would be jumping at the chance to hit the city. See the sights. Go to the club. Mingle. Get hot and sweaty under the bright lights. What's up with you, anyway?"

Shelby counted to ten. Then, she counted to five. And, two more, just because everything she wanted to say would incense him further.

A shitty start to what could have been a great day, had she been smart enough to drive herself to school. Too late now to wish she'd refused his offer of a ride this morning.

She always expected things would be better with Turner. That he'd be the kind of guy she knew—no, hoped—he could be. All her life she'd thought people were genuinely good, on the inside at least, even if their exterior needed a bit of polish. But the longer she stayed with him, the more she doubted that was true.

He seemed, as the song said, bad to the bone.

And she hated it.

And she was so damn tired of his petulant, obnoxious, bullying personality.

"Nothing is 'up with me' except I don't want to go to some smoky bar hours from here, just to be dragged around by you and your band of brothers. You know you'll all get drunk, and the girls will have to put up with every bit of the stupidity."

The last time she agreed to go on a group date to a club (which turned out to be a disgusting dive an hour downstate) every brother got wasted. Two got sick. One passed out. And Turner, who stayed on his feet, was so rude she wished he'd been violently ill, too.

"Fine. You don't want to go? I'm sure someone else'll want to have some fun with me."

They were just a few blocks from the entrance to the university. Traffic was, as usual, heavier near campus, so they'd slowed. He waved his hand in the air, ashes from the lit cigarette flying between them. One ember landed on the seat and burned a tiny hole in the gray upholstery. She didn't mention it; the new hole blended into the dozen already there.

"Are you threatening me?" Even an angel had her limits, and while she'd never considered herself angelic, she took some pride in having more than her share of patience. The conversation, however, had pushed her to the edge. "Because you'd better be sure that's what you want to do, if you're doing it."

"Sounds like you're the one threatening me, Shelby." He gunned the engine, pulled out into the oncoming traffic lane, and illegally passed a car stopped at the curb.

"The yellow lines—damn it, you're going to get us killed." She scanned the area, hoping to spot a patrol car. "Those double lines? Really?"

He tossed the butt out his window, huffed the last smoke from his lungs into her side of the car, and turned onto university property. "You used to be fun. I don't know what happened to you."

I smartened up, she thought. Swallowing her anger, Shelby concentrated on calming down.

Her first class this morning was Hemingway, with an essay quiz on a surprise topic. The professor never made the quizzes easy; he expected his students to analyze and interpret the writing.

She didn't ask if Turner was prepared for the class. It would be a waste of time.

"I'm sorry you feel that way." She searched the parking lot for an open space. He passed those that were deemed—in his fat head—too far a walk for a frat brother. She prayed they'd find an empty slot close to the building so she didn't have to listen to a tirade about how freshmen should have to park off campus, along with the jocks and brainiacs.

She'd been there. Done that. Heard it all—and hoped to not have to listen to his endless verbal diarrhea on the subject one more time.

"There!" She pointed. A battered Subaru Brat just backed out, leaving an opening near the walkway leading to the lecture hall.

Turner slid right in. When he turned the engine off, he had the manners to look her way. He winked. "Good one. We're right up close, the way we like to be."

He took the keys from the ignition. Bouncing them on a palm, he sighed.

"Listen, Shel, I don't want to fight with you." He could turn on the charm as if he were a faucet. His words were flawlessly delivered, but she saw behind the false sincerity. "We're both buggin' this morning, that stupid lit quiz has us in knots."

She was not in knots over school. Her issues were personal, and he was the cause of a fair share. Unless she gave in, at least on the face of it, he would never let her get to class without another dressing down. It was a lesson learned from experience, so she played the game.

A conciliatory nod. A phony smile. "You're right, we both need to chill. The professor can throw curveballs. Sometimes his essay questions are tough."

Turner snorted. "Guy's a jackass. He shouldn't even be teaching kindergarten, let alone college. Not an ounce of sense in that old head, and we're the ones paying for him doing a crap job."

The professor was brilliant. He'd received awards, written countless articles in literary journals, and had even published a few highbrow novels, but she kept her mouth closed. Her opinion was not worth sharing with the close-minded fool beside her.

"I've got to go." She reached for the door handle. He leaned over, placed his hand on hers and kept her from pushing it. "Turner, I've really got to go. Let me out."

He was so close she smelled his breath.

She'd have preferred to stick her face in a garbage can than breathe in the staleness wafting from between his lips. When he inclined closer, bringing his face inches from hers, she backed up. There wasn't much room in the car, but she put her spine against the seat and shook her head.

"No, please."

"Just a little kiss. You know, a kiss to make up?" He leered, dropping his gaze to the neckline of her dress where a hint of cleavage showed. "Isn't that what fighting is for? To have make up sex afterward?"

Revulsion turned the acid in her gut nearly volcanic. Between feeling two inches from a dirty ashtray and pretending his smarminess didn't disgust her, she was close to being sick. For real.

She pushed her hand down, hard. The door latch released and the door swung open.

Scrambling out of the car, she was aware her dress hiked up her thighs, but she didn't pause to yank it down. So what if he got an eyeful? Better to be away from him, regardless of the cost to her modesty.

"See you in class." She wanted to add *asshole* but just hurried toward the footpath. Behind her, a sarcastic snicker. She'd gotten away, but he'd managed to get the last word in, even if that word was non-verbal.

She wasn't surprised. He was used to having the upper hand, last word and final say…and she'd never questioned letting him have any of those things. Until now.

Something had changed in the past twenty-four hours. She wasn't sure what caused it, but suddenly she wasn't at all inclined to let the bad-boy fraternity hotshot walk all over her.

She shouldered the door to the redbrick building open. The halls were packed, but she threaded her way past clusters of students, straight for the hall where the Hemingway course took place.

Normally, she would have waited for Tania to show up before she entered the lecture hall. Today she went in and sat right in the front row. Front row—center.

Turner expected her to sit near the back on days when they had tests, so he could "peek" at her papers. He would be pissed when he saw where she was, but she didn't give a damn.

Let him be angry, and realize she wasn't going to put up with any more of his bullshit. This was a day that was long overdue, and she planned to enjoy every minute of it.

Chapter 15

"That wasn't as rough as I thought it would be." Tania hitched her backpack onto her right shoulder, adjusting the strap so it didn't cover the Greek letters embroidered on her sweater. It was something all sisters automatically did. "I figured he'd for sure ask us some out-there, existentialist baloney that only a philosophy major would be able to answer. And you—you'd get whatever he throws at us. You've got that literary brain thing going on. But me, an education major with a minor in fashion design? Some things are just over my head."

They filed out, nodding to the professor as they passed his desk. He'd already begun perusing the essays, stopping to read passages from a couple as he pushed them into the scuffed brown briefcase he carried everywhere.

In the hallway, Shelby bumped shoulders with her. "Don't sell yourself short, sister. Remember, you're the one who masters statistics like nobody's business. Heck, I'm more likely to get the finger chording right for the new Ramones riff solo than I am to find the bell curve on anything."

Just out the exit doors, they paused on the wide stone steps. Around them, kids going in all directions. Some entering for classes slated to begin in twenty minutes, while others, like them, glad to have fulfilled yet one more obligation on the college career ladder. The lecture hall had been chilly—probably to save the university's utility bill as well as discourage dozing during class—so standing in the sunshine was a welcome change.

"Chad helps me." Tania put a pair of round-lens sunglasses on. They made her look like a nearsighted insect, but none of the sisters had the heart to tell her.

Shelby turned her head, looking for her own sunglasses in her purse while she concealed a smile. She found them, a sensible pair of aviator-framed, tinted glasses she'd gotten on discount at Macy's last year. They were still in good shape and cut the sun's glare to a minimum. The drawback of having green eyes was the effect of light. A statistic she knew because it applied to her was that green-eyed people had less tolerance for bright light, which meant increased eye-induced headaches.

She put her glasses on. "Don't give him too much credit. You do the work, and get the grades. So, he helps. Big deal."

It was a big deal, having a guy who lifted his girlfriend up instead of tearing her down. So far, she hadn't known that luxury.

"I still wish I could wrap my head around obscure literary themes the way you do." They went down the steps and walked slowly toward the parking lot. "Tell me, what did you give the professor as your symbolism from *The Sun Also Rises*?"

The assignment had been to cite an example and discuss the inferred meaning of the author's using that item, event, or issue in the context of the novel. Her only struggle had been choosing a symbolic example to discuss. There were so many that selecting just one had been more difficult than writing the actual essay in the twenty allotted minutes.

"I went with the bullfighting, like everyone else probably did. I mean, it was so strong that choosing something else almost diminished the fight scenes."

Tania dumped her pack on the hood of her Pinto and leaned against the fender. "Go on, please."

"Well, Hemingway's use of bullfighting in the novel is symbolic of the relationship between the two sexes. He gives such raw energy and power to the fight that it can be likened to the sexual encounters between men and women. They are sometimes brutal, and frenzied, and often end with a victor. Symbolically, of course."

She put her pack beside the other and lifted her hair off her neck. The day had grown warm, and she wished she'd tied it up. Or maybe thinking about sex for the past half hour had heated her from inside. Who knew?

"It isn't always like that. Sex doesn't always have to be that way."

Unfortunately, the encounters she experienced with Turner had not been romantic, flying butterflies and soft music events. They were not brutal, and she'd been a willing participant, but his idea of lovemaking was in a car's back seat, rushed and not at all mutually satisfying.

"That's what I hear." A rueful smile. "Someday I'll find out. But hey, we're not talking about my sex life— or lack of one. Hemingway's symbolism is the discussion, remember? What did you write about?"

Tania closed her eyes and put a hand over her face. "Ugh. I chose the bullfight, too—no surprise, there—

but I wasn't half as deep as you were. By comparison, you're a lake and I'm a puddle, literarily speaking. I just hope my trite rambling gets me a B. That's all I need to stay on the side of academic excellence that the scholarship committee considers worth paying for, a solid B average."

"You'll get it. No worries." Turner was headed their way, moving across the lawn between the building and parking lot. She would rather stick a hot poker in her eye than have a second confrontation, so she picked up her backpack and went to the passenger door. It was unlocked, as usual. The key for the door locks was long lost, so they were always open. "Give me a lift back to my house? I need to pick up my car."

"Sure." Tania looked up, nodded to the lawn. "Turner's coming…"

"Yeah. Let's get the hell out of here before I have to talk to him, okay?" She slid into the car, slammed the door behind her, and was grateful when her friend jumped behind the wheel.

Tania started the engine, barely looking over her shoulder before she backed out. "You got it. The great escape, sister-style!"

Chapter 16

Shelby didn't expect her father to be home when they arrived. He was hardly there at all anymore, working late into the night and leaving with her when she went to early classes. It seemed with her mother gone, he hated the place.

Their footsteps were loud in the large house. Tania followed her into the kitchen, where they deposited their packs on the polished oak table. It shined, like everything else in the place.

A housekeeper came twice a week now, to dust, vacuum, and do the laundry. She brought flowers, too. The fresh bouquet of lilies in the cut-glass vase in the center of the table attested to the fact that Debbie had been by while Shelby was in class. Last night, drooping daisies filled the vase.

"Soda?" She went to the large side-by-side fridge and opened the right-hand door. Like everything else, the inside sparkled. No Tupperware containers filled with leftovers or half-eaten cakes sat on the glass shelves. Cans of soda lined a shelf at eye level. Below, bottles of Budweiser, her father's beverage of choice. "Tab? Or Coke?"

"Tab."

She took two cans out and let the door slap closed behind her as she handed one to Tania. They pulled the metal tabs, lifted the cans, and sipped. It was cold, and they enjoyed the treat without speaking for a minute.

"I love this stuff." Tania grinned, held the can up and gave it a Vanna White, Wheel of Fortune hand motion. "Better than buying a vowel or winning a car."

"It's my favorite, too, but I'm not so sure about the car thing. Although I think I'd rather win a boat."

"You've already got a hell-on-wheels car, remember?"

They headed for the stairs. The house was a split-level, so they passed the never-used-anymore-but-perpetually-dust-free living room on the left side of the hallway and the only-for-show dining room on the right. Before the ALS her parents had entertained in those rooms. Laughter had filled the house. Dinner parties had been lavish, often catered, and toasts had been made. If she closed her eyes, she could still hear the tinkle of flatware on china.

Memories. That's all that was left of that life.

Taking the beige, carpeted stairs two at a time, she led the way to her suite of rooms. Being an only child had its advantages, and one was having a wing of the house all to herself. Bedroom, en suite bathroom, and spare room for television, music, and study made life sweet.

Tania flopped down on the king-size bed, kicked off her Frye boots, and pulled her feet up onto the Laura Ashley comforter. She ran an appreciative hand across the stitching.

"I'm squished into a dorm room, and you've got your own apartment. What gives?"

Shelby opened the door to the massive walk-in closet, flipped the light switch on the wall, and went inside. "You know I want to live in the sorority house as badly as you do. At least you're not in your parents' house—you're out, on your own… Damn, I'd trade you any day of the week."

"Easy to say, when you're in the lap of luxury. You've never shared a room with two sisters or eaten chicken noodle soup four nights in a row because that's all your mother could afford to put on the table."

Tania's father had left right after her mom got pregnant with her younger sister. The family struggle had made all three girls determined to make better lives for themselves—and their mom. So far, two had full scholarships and the youngest was an honor roll student in high school.

Forgetting the disparity between their childhoods was not hard because Shelby did not put any real emphasis on money. But those who had never had any, or had done without, had an entirely different point of view. Tania never forgot her background.

They were headed to the racquetball court, so she changed from the t-shirt dress into a pair of sweats with a tank top under an off-the-shoulder sweatshirt. Every item had the Greek letters on it. She pulled a matching outfit from the stack on the shelf, walked out of the closet, and put the clothes on the bed.

Her favorite spot had always been the window seat overlooking the back yard, so she sat there now. She pulled her feet onto the padded bench and wrapped her arms around her knees. "You're right, I don't know what any of that's like. And I'm sorry you do."

Tania took the clothes and went into the bathroom. She didn't close the door, so they spoke while she was in there.

"It's not your fault, so don't be sorry." The toilet

flushed, and the water in the sink ran for a moment. "It's just the way things work out, is all. Yeah, I want to be in the house with the sisters, but I'm just glad to have my shoebox of a room in MacDuff Hall." She emerged, adjusting the sweatshirt. "But don't let your guard down; I'd jump at the chance to trade places with you and live in this—" She spread her arms wide and smiled. "For a while."

"It's not as great as you think. Erma Bombeck, and the grass is greener, remember?"

"I hear you. I still wouldn't refuse to test the grass, though."

"Ready?" She drained the last of her soda and tossed the empty into the wicker wastebasket beside her desk. "Let's go smack the ball around for a while. Get out the aggression."

Tania tossed her can in also, and they went into the hallway. At the top of the stairs, she said, "So you and Turner had another argument?"

Holding up her hand like a cop stopping traffic, she took the stairs at a near run. "Don't even say that asshole's name. I swear, I must be the biggest idiot on campus for putting up with his garbage for this long."

They left through the front door, taking two rackets from the coat closet as they passed.

Tania patted her on the shoulder. "Nope. I'm sure there's a bigger idiot on campus. You're not getting the prize on that one. So, are you going to give me a ride in your little blue car, or what?"

Chapter 17

The whole drive to school Shelby wondered if her ghostly guest would put in an appearance. Surprisingly, thinking about that instead of the clutch and shift made driving less stressful. She didn't grind a gear once, and only realized it went so well when she parked outside the Physical Education building on the lower end of campus.

Tania had gotten into the passenger seat without a problem, so she worried needlessly that her pal Joey (she'd accepted his presence in her life—most particularly, her car—so calling him by name, even in her mind, seemed the right thing to do) would boot anyone other than himself riding shotgun.

They took their rackets and got out of the sleek car.

It was the first time she'd been in it that she hadn't hated the thing.

"This has got to be the most adorable set of wheels I've ever seen." Tania stood back, surveying the Cobra. It was parked under a tree and took up less than half the space allotted between the painted white lines on the pavement. "I never thought I'd ride in anything like this, really."

Shelby tried to appreciate the car, looking at it the way she knew the other woman did. And the other sisters, who'd all commented that it was too cute for words. Now, she viewed with a less critical attitude.

It was definitely nothing to sneer at. There were only a few made, and if this one hadn't been abandoned in a barn for two decades, it would have remained out of reach for her father. He was fulfilling his dream by giving her the car, and while she loved him for that, it was awkward. What he yearned for wasn't anything she'd ever wanted.

The big engine and sleek design were not at all her thing. And yes, she could see it was sweet—she wasn't blind, for heaven's sake!—but she still didn't like it.

Part of her wished she could give the damn thing to Tania. Swap cars. Swap lives.

"Me, either." She gave the racket in her hand a test swing. It sliced the air with a satisfying *whoosh*. "I think I'll have to trade it for something more snow-worthy when the weather changes. I don't see me driving this through even one snowfall."

They headed for the building. "You've got a point. Too easy to end up off the road in something that small."

Remembering how she'd driven into the apple orchard, she giggled. "You have no idea."

Tania opened the door and held it, letting her pass through first. Immediately the scent of sweat assailed her, a warm, almost tangible cloud that made her anxious to get on the court they'd reserved.

The hallway was packed. A few familiar faces, so she nodded a couple of times as they made their way to the check-in counter.

Forgetting the car for a moment, she scanned the space to make certain there was no sign of Turner. There wasn't, but before she put her mind back on where she was going, she bumped into someone.

"Oh! I'm sorry, I didn't—oh, hi." The girl she'd nearly knocked down wasn't a stranger. She wasn't a friend, either, but at least she was smiling. "I know you, don't I?"

"We've met. Last semester, remember? I rushed the sorority for a while…" The words trailed off.

Shelby saw a sheen of tears in the other's eyes. Fragmented tidbits about the girl's story drifted into her head, but she couldn't remember exactly what the deal was. Or why she hadn't finished rushing.

"Right, I remember you." Flashing the smile that she hoped would make the misty eyes disappear, she added, "But I've got to admit; I'm terrible with names. It's amazing that I remember my own, even."

"Caroline Reed."

"Oh, right—Caro, isn't it?"

A brighter smile and a nod. "Yes, that's it. I really regret not finishing the rush process. I always dreamed of being in a sorority."

The crowd around them grew. They were still pretty much in the doorway, with people going in and out on either side. And every minute she stood talking meant a minute less on the court, so Shelby tried to wrap things up.

"Hey, life gets in the way sometimes." A little shrug. "I've got to run—good seeing you. And, really, think about rushing again. We all thought you'd be a valuable asset to the sisterhood. See you!"

"I will, thanks. Bye!"

Tania was already waiting outside court number five.

As she hurried through the crush of bodies, Shelby wished she wasn't so pressed for time. There had been a connection during the rush period, and she'd been sad when the prospective sister pulled out before bids were offered.

She hoped the other would rush again. Greek involvement wasn't for everyone, but it had completely enriched her own life. Caro looked as if she could use a bit of sisterly camaraderie.

Chapter 18

"I have to say this, and I don't know how you're going to take it, but I felt something in the car." Tania shrugged out of her sweatshirt, tossed it to the floor beside the door, and looked her right in the eyes. "Really, I felt something…"

Shelby's heart tripped.

"What do you mean, *something*?"

When the door closed behind them, every sound from the hallway disappeared. They were cocooned in the space, insulated from everything else.

It was one of her favorite things about the game. There weren't many sports where the world faded away. She often booked court time to play alone, just to block everything out and smack the little ball off the far wall. Total stress relief, without having to explain why she hit the ball as hard as she could, or why she wanted to hit it harder next time.

They walked onto the court.

She watched her friend bounce the ball off the floor a few times. A furrow had appeared on her brow, and she knew Tania was choosing her words carefully. And it almost frightened her. She wasn't at all sure she wanted anyone else to "see" her new friend. On the other hand, she wished someone would, so she'd know for certain she wasn't losing her marbles.

Finally, a shrug. "I don't know how to explain it."

"Try."

That got a raised eyebrow, but she didn't back down.

"Please, try. What's the *something* you felt in the car?"

"It's stupid, really. That's a sports car, built to go fast and not at all cute and cuddly, but I felt something, I don't know, soft in the car."

She nearly laughed out loud. "Soft?"

Tania rolled her eyes. "I said I don't know how to explain it…it was a feeling. Just that I expected to be blown away by speed or some kind of weird power thing, but I felt safe. Yeah, there was lots of male energy—sorry, it's a total testosterone burst on wheels—but along with that I just felt…like I said, safe. Warm. Like the car wasn't going to let anything bad happen."

"You do realize it's a *car*, right?"

"I do." Tania threw the ball in the air and served. It bounced off the far wall and headed back to where they stood, rackets at the ready. If they didn't finish the conversation now, they never would. Well-suited for each other, they played hard and fast—with lots of grunting but virtually no talking.

Shelby returned the ball. "And you think it's capable of not letting anything bad happen? Really?"

Another smack off the wall.

"Yep. It's not just a car—it's got a personality, I think. And a definite energy about it." She whacked it with the racket, sending it flying across the court. "Real energy—like, almost more energy inside the car than under its hood."

Chapter 19

Joey leaned against the back wall while Shelby and Tania played. Watching them run across the racquetball court was no hardship. The view was ideal; every time Shelby swung or rushed the ball it was as if she were coming directly to him.

He'd made himself invisible for two reasons. If they saw him standing where they aimed, it would be a major distraction. And the ability to watch without detection…he didn't do it too often, but it certainly came in handy now.

Alfonso popped in behind the two women. He stood for a minute, looking from one to the other. A low whistle.

"I don't need to ask how it's hanging, amigo." He sauntered across the court. The ball bounced eighteen inches to his right, but he didn't flinch. When he reached the far end, he turned and leaned against the wall. They were nearly shoulder to shoulder. "If anyone had told me when I was alive that I'd be watching this after I died, I would never have believed it."

"Me, either." He wanted to cheer when Shelby bent nearly double and returned an almost impossible shot. "Not as good as heaven, but not too shabby."

"Ever think heaven might not be that great?" Alfonso met his gaze and raised a questioning brow.

"Never did give it much thought. I just figure it's

got to be better than hell." He paused, weighing his words. If not now, when? "Is that why you're not in a rush to move on?"

"It shows, huh?"

His interest was on the golden-haired beauty, but he looked over at his friend. "I don't want to pry, or worse, piss you off because hey, you're my only friend in this never-never land between dead and alive—"

"Oh, we're dead, all right."

"Yeah, I get that. I meant—"

"I know what you meant. I'm just having some fun with you."

"I'm not trying to be rude, but don't you want to go to heaven?" When it came down to it, Joey didn't have much to lose so he went all in. "And if that doesn't annoy you, do you mind telling me how old you are?"

Alfonso didn't take umbrage. A lazy smile spread across his face. "Took you long enough to ask."

"Like I said, I didn't want to pry."

"But you've been wondering. Trying to calculate in your head, asking yourself just how old this Mexican ghost really is." He tapped the unlit cigarette against the palm of one hand. "You're a smart fellow. How old do you peg me for?"

The girls were still going hard at the ball. Shelby's sneakers squeaked against the hardwood flooring every time she changed direction. Tania's exertion expressed itself in a soft *huff* with each swing.

He had gotten used to hearing both sounds.

"I don't want to insult you." Had he been mortal, Joey would have dodged the ball Tania sent his way. It bounced off the wall barely two inches from his right ear. "But I know you've got a lot of years on you."

"Yeah, I'd say I have a few. Two hundred—plus."

"When you died? How old were you?" Joey gauged him to be about forty by the wrinkled forehead, worn hands and knowing expression in his eyes.

"Twenty-four."

He tried to hide his shock. "Your family…"

"All dead." An appreciative smile when Tania saved what appeared to be a doomed serve. "They went to heaven, I'm sure. I haven't seen them here, in this between place. Not many here, actually."

The game was nearly over and he would have liked to watch Shelby without distraction but he was compelled to ask.

"Don't you want to see them again? Your family in heaven?"

Alfonso put the cigarette between his lips. Chomped down on the end with his teeth. Shook his head. "I wasn't a real good man in life, amigo. I'm not sure my family would be happy to see me, even in heaven. I'm sure they think—if they think about me at all—that I'm in hell, where I deserve to be. A man does what he's told to do when he goes to war, but that doesn't mean it ain't counted against him at judgment time."

"Acts of war shouldn't count." He wasn't sure if he believed that, but there was no harm in trying to soothe the other's soul.

"Oh, they should. I think that's why I'm here, because of what happened when I took part in the uprising." He shot Joey a look. "But you, amigo? I still haven't figured out what you could've done to land yourself in this deadly limbo."

He couldn't, either. If limbo was for every so-called bad boy, the place would be filled to capacity. But it was desolate. Two lonely ghosts wandering around, not another specter in sight.

They stood silently for a while. Watched the two women run across the court. Smiled when they saved a ball. Nodded when they congratulated each other. Saw friendly competition without any pretense.

Finally Alfonso spoke. "Best seats in the house."

"They are."

"The one with hair the color of wheat in the sunshine—is she your girl?"

Joey snorted. "I wish. A guy's got to have a pulse to get a girl like that."

The ball slammed the wall near their shoulders.

"Good thing we gave up pulses years ago." Alfonso smirked, pointing to the ball as it came whizzing toward them again. "That thing comes faster than musket fire. If I weren't dead, I'd keel over from fright."

Chapter 20

"Are you sure you don't want a lift? I don't mind dropping you at the dorm."

They'd played so long the sun's presence was just a single orange band above the trees at the far edge of campus. Smoky purples and blues, dark and sultry, showed their colors overhead. A handful of early stars twinkled.

"Nah, it's no big deal to walk. Thanks, anyway." Tania held her racket loosely in one hand while she wiped her neck with the heel of the other. "I've got to get back, jump in the shower, and get ready. Chad's meeting me at the library."

Shelby had psychology chapters to read. Her plan had been to study at home, but the very idea of being all alone in that quiet house dragged her spirits down.

A spur-of-the-moment suggestion. "What are you guys doing about dinner? I'm going home to shower and change, then going to the library with my Abnormal Psych text. How about I grab a pizza from Carmine's on the way back? We can meet on the wall, have a bite before locking ourselves in between the stacks of books."

When her friend hesitated, she added, "My treat. I got some cash from my dad for my birthday. Hey, I'm in the mood for a pepper-and-onion pie, and I can't eat a whole one by myself. Say you'll eat with me. Chad,

93

too."

A slow smile. Tania probably realized she stretched the truth but was cool enough to simply agree. "I'd like that. Chad will, too. I planned to make him split a sandwich with me in the dining hall, and you know what that means."

Shelby shuddered. "Soggy white bread. Ugh!"

"Exactly. So, what time should we meet you? He's supposed to be here at five."

"Perfect. That's enough time to get ready, pick up the grub, and get back."

The white brick wall outside the Fine Arts Building was the meet-and-greet hangout spot. Mostly Greeks sat there, watching campus life from the prized position. Occasionally a pothead would try to crash, but no one ever got far. There were enough sisters and brothers hanging out there at any given time to squelch anyone's idea of infringing on what they considered their territory. Greek traditions went deep on campus; the wall had been passed down from generation to generation, house to house.

Tania turned for the walkway leading to the dorms with a small wave. "Be there—"

"Or be square," Shelby finished.

The car felt empty when she got behind the wheel. No Tania. No Joey. Just her…and the thoughts she'd been pushing aside all day.

Ignoring Turner wasn't going to make him go away. She had to deal with him, and she knew that. She just wasn't sure how to deal.

He was an ass. No disputing it. But he did have some good qualities. Occasionally he treated her decently.

Occasionally? What the hell was she thinking?

There was no radio in the car, so she hummed. Off-key and sort of breathlessly, but it gave her something to do besides dwell on the upcoming clash with the on-again, off-again boyfriend. Because, like it or not, there was going to be a confrontation. And knowing his inflated ego, it was going to be messy.

Halfway home, her otherworldly traveler arrived. She hadn't been looking at the passenger seat, so she had no idea how he managed to suddenly appear. When he hummed along with the old melody she was mindlessly ruining, she smiled.

"You're back."

"I am. And I like your choice of music."

Her heart warmed. "My mother used to sing that to me when I was little. At bedtime, mostly, but other times, too." She glanced over. It had grown darker but she could see a half-smile on his face. "She had a great voice and could carry a tune. Me? Not so much."

"You were doing just fine." He paused, then asked, "Do you know who sang the song?"

It was unexpected. No one ever heard her hum the song, so no one asked about it. Now that he had, her throat felt much too tight to answer, so she nodded.

His tone was gentle. "The Platters were my favorite group. I actually saw them once, down in Brooklyn. Great show."

This was the first time he'd offered up information about his life. Shelby didn't let him off the hook.

"So, did you have a girlfriend? Back when…well, you know."

How to say it? *Before you died* sounded harsh, but it was in her head. Conversation with a ghost wasn't without pitfalls, something she had just learned by almost putting her foot—sneaker and all—into her mouth.

He didn't take offense. A fast head shake and pursed lips before he answered, "No girlfriend, although I did take someone to the concert. I think she wanted to see the show, and didn't care who she went with."

"I'm sorry."

"Hey, it's just a fact of life. She was a nice girl, but her parents wouldn't have liked her getting involved with a guy like me."

It didn't sound like much had changed over the years.

"What do you mean?" She signaled, turning onto her street. Traffic was light. Down the block, she saw the guy who lived in the house next door to theirs had just pulled into his driveway. Slowing ever-so slightly, she waited for his reply.

"You know how it is."

Her neighbor took two brown paper grocery bags from the back seat of his Buick, kicked the door closed with a foot, and headed toward his front steps. She watched, waiting until he was on the stoop before she sped up and pulled into her own driveway.

"I don't, actually." She shut off the car. There wasn't a lot of time to dawdle, but talking with Joey beat the quiet house. "You seem like a nice guy. And you're not a horror to look at."

He grinned. "Thanks. I think."

Heat bloomed on her cheeks, but she pushed on. "You know what I mean. I'm just trying to say it's hard to believe a guy like you didn't have a girlfriend."

He dragged in a deep breath. For a wild moment, she wondered why a ghost would need oxygen at all, but she let the thought disappear. What did it matter, anyway?

He met her gaze, and she was mesmerized by the sincerity in his dark eyes.

"I could ask you the same thing. A beautiful girl like you, with those long legs and miles of thick, golden hair…and your personality makes your killer looks take the back seat." He looked behind them. Shrugged. A grin that could charm a snake from its basket. "That is, if there *was* a back seat. But you get my gist. A pretty lady like you, without a boyfriend? That doesn't make sense."

The move to divert attention from himself was slick.

Shelby shook her head. "You're wrong. I do have a—ah, I have a boyfriend." She nearly choked on the word but technically, for now, she did.

He leaned back against the seat with a firm headshake. "Don't try to feed me a line, babe. I see more than you think I do."

Her hackles rose. "But I do have a boyfriend. His name is Turner—"

"Walker. And that guy's no boyfriend. Hell, he's hardly human."

Chapter 21

Not knowing the rules of the game wore him down. Constantly wondering how to get past this stage seemed the final insult. How could an all-powerful being treat people this way? Granted, he wasn't perfect, but no one deserved to wander the earth forever.

He didn't want to end up like Alfonso, eternally roaming between worlds with no hope of moving forward.

College life—the existence he had been denied—surrounded him. Clusters of young men and women doing the thing he could not do. They were living. Toting backpacks. Learning. Growing. Holding hands.

The futility of his existence tore a hole in Joey's heart.

No one could hear him, so he threw his head back and shouted to the sky.

"Damn you! Just damn you, St. Peter, for leaving me here to rot this way!" His voice caught ,but he pulled strength from his fury and refused to give in to despair. "You're a chickenshit saint, that's what you are. You don't have the guts to face me—how the hell can a guy know what he's supposed to do when you won't let me near your Pearly Gates?"

Hank, free of the security kiosk, strolled his way.

Had he been alive he'd surely have gotten a reprimand for his behavior. He'd have drawn attention from anyone within earshot. But the guard didn't even slow down, although Joey stood right in his path.

If he were solid, they would have collided. Hank passed through him without even knowing he'd done so. He may have felt a fleeting chill, but even that was unlikely.

The fact he had no effect at all on the world around him ratcheted up the overall frustration level.

"This sucks! Do you hear me, St. Peter? This sucks—and you should let me up there so we can talk this shitty thing out." He raised a fist and waved it above his head. "I demand entrance—now!"

A loud *whoosh* and he felt sucked into a swirling vortex. There was no sense of up or down, right or left. His equilibrium was gone, and he floated in a cloud of white.

Holy shit, he thought as something soft touched his cheek. What the hell have I gone and done now?

Just as suddenly as he was lifted, his feet touched something solid. The white disappeared, replaced by nothing he'd ever seen—not even in his wildest imaginings.

He turned, slowly. Rotated in a complete circle. Then, he did it a second time.

Everywhere, brilliant bursts of color. A riotous world of hues. He looked up. Purple and magenta, with teal streaks. At his feet, some yellow blended with pink. Splotches everywhere, as if some giant had shaken a paint brush and splattered everything in its reach.

"Pretty, isn't it?"

Joey turned to the voice. It was familiar, but he couldn't quite place it.

"Uh, yeah. Very colorful."

That brought a grin from the black-haired, middle-aged, slightly overweight guy who appeared from behind a two-story wall of periwinkle. He was dressed in a skintight black leather jumpsuit with rhinestone-studded cuffs and matching collar. A sheer baby blue scarf tucked in near his neck. Polished white leather boots with the letters TCB embossed onto their toes completed the ensemble.

Joey had never seen anything—or anyone—like it.

"What? You expected white clouds, maybe? A couple of white-robed angels playing harps?"

"Where am I?"

"Exactly where you're supposed to be." He paused. Waved a finger through the air, sending a cascade of color across the already saturated landscape. Diamonds glittered from rings on every finger. The biggest, on his pinky finger, was surrounded by rubies. "No, wait, that's not right, is it? You *were* where you're supposed to be. Now, you're where you demanded to be."

Oh, boy.

He swallowed. Could it be?

"You're St. Peter?"

The roundish man separated his arms and twisted to the side, one foot stretched far in front of the other. He circled one arm and wiggled his pelvis. Then he pointed and said, "That's right—St. Peter, at your service!"

Chapter 22

He'd had a long time to contemplate heaven. Nothing prepared him for this.

St. Peter settled onto a padded navy-blue plush sofa. Behind him, a sagging white-picket fence.

They had been staring at each other for about five minutes.

All the anger he'd harbored had vanished. There was no impulse to scream at the injustice of his situation. Quite simply, Joey had been stunned into silence.

A plate of sandwiches appeared—out of thin, multi-colored air—on the sofa. St. Peter picked up the plate and held it out.

"Peanut butter and banana. Want one? Trust me, they're good."

"No, thanks."

"Suit yourself. But don't say I didn't give you a chance." He put the plate down, chose a sandwich from the stack, and took a bite. A satisfied, belly-shaking groan. "Mmm mmm, but that is one whole lotta love."

His mind had to be playing tricks on him.

"Are you sure you're *the* St. Peter? You know, the one who decides who gets into heaven, and who doesn't?"

Another bite. "I'm your guy." He swallowed, then gave a lopsided grin. A corner of his upper lip lifted higher than the other. "It's no heartbreak hotel, but welcome to my world."

Joey couldn't shake the feeling he recognized this guy—and not as a saint, either.

Waving to the fence, he asked, "And I'm supposed to believe those are the Pearly Gates?"

"You know, you've got a suspicious mind. It's not like we're in the ghetto or anything." Pointing to the tips of the fence posts, he said, "Don't be cruel, judging the place like that. See right there? On every fencepost, a pearl. And not just any pearl, either. Oh, no. Those beauties? Straight out of blue Hawaii. Put that on your blue suede shoes and bossa nova."

There were pearls—big, fat, shiny ones— embedded into the wood. Still, something seemed off.

He waved his arms. The squishiness of the overstuffed red velveteen chair he occupied made movement difficult, but he managed to gesture to their surroundings.

"And you expect me to believe this is the gateway to heaven?"

The man opposite shoved the last bite of the first sandwich into his mouth and chewed. He swallowed, then licked three fingers. All as unhurriedly as if he had all the time in the world.

When he met Joey's gaze, he shrugged. "Look, you asked to come here, so don't treat me like a hound dog. This is heaven—or as close as you're going to get for now. And if you keep pushing, we're going to have to jailhouse rock—and to be honest, I'm in no mood for that."

Jailhouse Rock.

No. It couldn't be.

Could it?

He knew it was impolite but he pointed anyway. "You're…ah, you're…"

The twinkle in the other man's eyes gave him away. He knew he'd been recognized, and by the way he grinned, he was pleased.

"St. Peter." He pointed to the tips of his boots. "Taking care of business. And I know you're anxious so why don't we just get down to it? You're all shook up—I saw that by the way you were screaming down there." He jerked his chin to the pink-and-yellow blend at their feet. "The way I see it, you're lonesome tonight. And every night—for about two decades. You've found someone—a sweet, pretty little teddy bear—and you want to say, 'love me tender' but you can't because you're—well, because you're a big hunk of love who realizes it's now or never."

In some convoluted way that he did not entirely understand, the guy made sense.

Joey leaned forward, struggling to pull free of the man-eating chair. He put his elbows on his knees and clasped his hands together. "Can you help me? I don't know what I'm supposed to do to get into this place. Worse, now that I've met Shelby, I don't want to go to heaven. I want to stay with her—but what do I have to do to get my life back?"

"Surrender."

"Excuse me?"

St. Peter sighed as he reached for a second sandwich. "You can't help falling in love. Shelby? You're her good luck charm. You'll know what to do. Don't leave her father crying in the chapel. When the time comes, recognize the devil in disguise and send him way down."

So he'd been right. Shelby was the link between his death and…well, wherever he was.

There *had* to be more. "That's all you can tell me?"

"That's it." He took a bite of the sandwich and groaned. Holding it out, he asked, "Sure you don't want one for the road?"

"No, thanks. I'm not a banana kind of guy."

"You don't know what you're missing." Sighing, he contemplated the sandwich for a long moment. Then he met Joey's gaze. "Look, you've obviously got a burning love for the girl. It'll be all right. You're more than you think you are, believe me."

He stood, holding the sandwich as if it were made of something precious, and held out his free hand. Joey followed his lead, standing and putting his right hand out to shake.

"I hate to cut this short, but our time together is over for now." Their hands connected, and energy sizzled between them. The other man smiled when the colors around them began to swirl.

Joey heard six words as he was sucked into time.

St. Peter has left the building.

Chapter 23

Shelby was a few minutes late arriving at the wall, but Chad and Tania didn't seem to mind. Unlike so many other couples, whose public displays of affection sometimes bordered on the criminal, they were engaged, not in physical activity but in an intellectual dance that had both smiling.

"Didn't mean to keep you. The line at Carmine's was super long." She put the box down, handed out napkins and paper plates. She'd brought sodas, as well, and left them beside the pizza box. "*Mangia.*"

They each took a slice and began to eat.

Chad smiled at a couple walking by. Tania nodded to a girl from one of her classes. They both said, "Hey" to a group of runners jogging past.

"You two know everyone on campus." Shelby laughed. "I was worried about being late, but you probably didn't even notice, waving to all who pass as if you're a couple of celebrities."

"You're funny." Tania dabbed her lips with the paper napkin. "We've been practicing statistical theory on real-life subjects." She lowered her voice and leaned forward. "But don't tell anyone."

"Why would I tell anyone?"

Chad gazed at his girlfriend with an expression that made Shelby wish someone would look at her that way. "Because we're discussing the probability the couples who pass will either stay together through the end of semester, break up, or become victims to the free love mentality."

"Chad says he can spot the free lovers from across the quad. And he's right. He pointed out a couple just before you got here who, I have it on very good inside information, do actually have an open relationship."

She reached for a second slice of pizza. She took a bite, chewed, then asked, "How do you know? That he's right, I mean. No disrespect, Chad, but that's a kind of personal thing, to know if a couple is fooling around—with other people. So, how do you know?"

Since her boyfriend was busy eating, Tania answered. "He picked out a couple who have rooms on the floor above mine. It's no big secret that both of them do the Thursday night, after sours low-crawl with different people. It's practically a twisted joke, their almost-real relationship, in the dorm. There's no way Chad could've known about it."

She paid more attention to the people passing. She knew some, so nodded or waved, but focused on figuring out what kind of signs people gave off. When she saw a guy with long hair pull a face behind a preppie chick's back, she poked Tania in the side with her elbow.

"Those two. They're not making the full semester."

"Agreed." Chad picked up the empty pizza box and carried it to a nearby wire trash can. When he returned, he added, "I'm not sure they're going to make it through the night."

"Don't!" Tania put a hand up when he opened his mouth. She laughed as she warned him. "Don't you dare sing that hokey country western song. So help me

God, I will go to the library without you and hide in the stacks if you embarrass me here with your dubious singing skills."

"I'm better than she gives me credit for—especially when it comes to honky-tonk country songs. It's one of my special talents."

He directed his comment to Shelby, who merely shrugged. It wasn't her place to advise on public singing demonstrations.

His true talent was keeping her sister happy. The grin he shot Tania preceded a quick kiss on the cheek. Again, she wondered when anyone would be so sweet to her.

Never, she thought. It wasn't negative thinking, just the truth.

Okay, so maybe it was a little bit of negativity creeping into her mind, but it had been a long day. And it had started so terribly, with Turner's foolish antics.

"Not for me to judge who's in tune or out." She hopped down. It was a jeans-and-sweater evening, so she brushed her hands down her thighs and wiped off her butt. The wall was clean; it was just habit. "Who's ahead in this statistical dating adventure? Are you keeping score?"

"We are, actually." He reached into the pocket of his jeans and pulled out a folded bill, which he pushed into Shelby's right hand. "And I won the bet, so I'm buying us all dinner."

When she tried to protest, he waved her off.

"He's telling the truth." Tania drained the last bit of Tab from the can before she jumped down off the ledge. Squeezing the can in one hand, she said, "He's winning. Big time. Let him buy dinner—I'm never going to hear the end of how I can't predict compatibility. Statistically, of course. Our own compatibility quotient is easy to calculate."

He leaned in, kissed Tania on the nose, then shot Shelby a grin.

"Just so you know, I'm on the lookout for you, Shel." He winked. "A guy who's worthy of your time and energy. Statistically speaking, a guy like that is out there somewhere. Just want you to know, I've got my eyes peeled for the guy."

What could she say?

"Thanks. I, ah, I definitely appreciate your keeping my interests in mind like that."

The trio walked up the library steps. He walked in between, his arm around Tania's shoulders. He held her books, leaving her hands free.

"Hey, he should be taking care of you." Tania gazed up at her man, who winked, before she held her hand out. A round solitaire in a gold princess setting sparkled on her finger. "It happened two minutes before you got here, and no one else knows yet, but Chad is going to be your brother-in-law! He asked me to marry him!"

Chapter 24

Shelby was glad to have a quiet moment to herself on the ride home. So much had happened, in such a short amount of time that letting her mind relax was good. Necessary, even.

Driving the new car already came without effort. It was so compact, with everything close at hand—and foot—it practically felt custom made for her. Clutch and gas were side by side, the stick shift almost brushed her thigh and the dash was blessedly clear of any unnecessary clutter. No gauges she didn't understand, nothing to take her mind from the pleasure of effortlessly tooling along.

Her father, and everyone else, was right. The Cobra was a honey.

"Your shifting is smooth as silk stockings."

It didn't bother her that Joey just appeared. The peace had been nice, but this was better.

"Hmm?"

Just a few miles from the house, and suddenly she didn't want to go home. If her father was there, he'd be asleep. And if he wasn't, she would be alone. Again. At least in the car, she had company. Of a sort.

"You know, silk stockings." He sighed, closed his eyes, and ran a hand through the air in front of him. The outline of a leg, or a woman's bottom, she couldn't be sure which. Whatever it was, the memory brought a satisfied smile. "So smooth, sexy…"

"Ah, no. I have no idea how silk stockings feel." Her mother had never been one to overdress. Long, flowing maxi dresses and knee-length skirts paired with knee-high boots were her style. "I'm more a L'eggs kind of girl, myself."

He turned toward her. Opened his eyes. Raised a brow. "L'eggs?"

"That's right. You know, pantyhose. They come in a little plastic egg—like the ones kids get on Easter. Except there's no candy inside, just a squished up pair of nylon pantyhose."

"I can't claim to not know my way around a pair of nylons—I mean, what guy hasn't seen stockings? But *pantyhose*? Are they stockings in eggs?"

She had no idea when pantyhose were invented, but even if they were around in 1963—which she of course, being born that year, did not know one way or the other—Joey obviously hadn't been intimate with any woman who wore them.

The chance to startle him was a gift. Nothing she could ever do could compare to his just showing up the way he had. *Ta da! I'm your friendly poltergeist!* But giving him a taste of the time he'd invaded had to be interesting. More appealing by far than an empty shell of a home.

"Let me explain a few things." She drove past her street. Better to talk with someone…and, ghostliness aside, Joey was a good conversationalist. "You don't mind, do you?"

"Please. I seem to have missed certain things. I'd appreciate any tips you can give me."

This was going to be fun.

"I've seen stockings—although I've never personally worn them. I have, however, worn pantyhose."

"I'm already lost."

"Let me find you." Talking with him was comfortable. His laid-back attitude, non-confrontational cool vibes made her loose. She didn't consider every word before opening her mouth, the way she did with Turner.

Ugh. Forget the asshole, she reminded herself.

"Nowadays, women take shortcuts. The old garter belt, girdle, two stockings thing is history. We just don't have time, energy, or the obligation to conform to a man's view of what a woman should look like."

"Interesting." His tone held a note of amusement.

There were few cars on the road. Less stopping, so less shifting. She pushed the speed on the empty, straight stretch. A tiny chill from the night air came through the open windows.

"The pantyhose take care of all of those things, in one little plastic egg, as I said."

"You still haven't explained exactly what they are, although I do have a mind picture." He shook his head, and she stifled a giggle. It was clear what he thought of the image he'd conjured. "I really hope I'm wrong, but I've got this sneaking suspicion you're going to confirm my thoughts…"

"Panties. Stockings. All in one. Is that what you're seeing?"

Joey put a hand over his eyes. A groan tore from him, frustration and disappointment all rolled into a single deep, masculine sound. Her body reacted to the groan, her nipples coming to attention beneath her

111

clothes and something tightening low in her belly.

"Maybe you shouldn't tell me anymore. I'm not sure I'm ready for it."

She laughed, something she didn't do nearly enough. Back in the day, before her life fell apart, she laughed all the time. Now it was usually a social move, something she did because it was expected. This joy, though, was real.

No pretense. No pushing past a barrier of grief. No complying in order to keep from becoming the victim of another's frustration.

"Oh, come on...a guy like you? You're not scared of a lady's undergarments, are you?"

He took his hand off his face. The half-smile he wore turned handsome to heartstopping. It was good she was driving. If not for the car and the road, she might have embarrassed herself and started to drool.

"Not normally, no. But like I said, I'm old school. I'm used to a woman wearing a dress. Stockings. Heels. And if a guy is lucky enough to, you know..."

Her mouth was suddenly dry. "Know what?"

"Well, if a guy is lucky enough to get close to a lady...maybe close enough to run a hand down her back when he kisses her...cup her...ah, hell..."

There was a scenic viewpoint of distant mountains just outside town. During the day, tourists snapped photos. After dark, stoners went to smoke weed. And lovers went to make out. The view of the moon and stars was spectacular, although mostly ignored by the occupants of the cars parked along the edge of the embankment.

Only one car was in the parking area. Shelby drove to the other side of the dirt lane, angled the car in so they had a sensational view and then turned the key to the off position. For a few seconds, the only sound was the engine as it cooled.

The interior of the car was very tight. They sat nearly shoulder to shoulder, so when she turned to face him, her hair practically brushed his shoulders.

Joey hung an elbow out the open window. He tapped his fingertips against the door frame when he turned to meet her gaze.

"You were saying?" Playing with fire, she thought. A bolt of pure lust shot up her spine and she waved common sense off. "About men…and women…and what goes on between them…?"

Chapter 25

It had been so long since he was near a woman he almost didn't know how to act. He'd never been shy around the opposite sex but now...well, now was a whole new ball game. The rules had changed over the years. And so had his status as a human being. Two strikes, definitely.

The rides in the Cobra with Shelby were one thing; she concentrated on driving while he tried not to frighten her into wrapping them around a light post. Sure, he'd considered putting a hand on her knee or running his fingers through that curtain of honey gold hair that flew in the breeze, but he hadn't followed his craving. His instincts. Aside from the one time when he almost put his hand on hers over the gear shift, he had maintained a distance.

Parking in a secluded, romantic spot gave him ideas. Lots of ideas. Strong ones that made it hard to stay on his side of the car.

The moon was picture-perfect, full and round.

"A Honeymooners moon." He jutted his chin to the huge white orb hanging low before them. It seemed to almost fill the sky above the overlook, a solid circle of light just outside the windshield.

"Come again?"

Jackie Gleason and Ed Sullivan were the best reasons for owning a television. They entertained without preaching, the ways newscasters were wont to do. It was enough that they lived in a turbulent, post-Hitler world. He didn't need to be reminded it wasn't all flowers and rainbows.

So he watched the Honeymooners once a week. And Ed Sullivan with Topo Gigio on Sunday nights. Too much television, perhaps, but others must have a worse habit with it.

"You know, Alice and Ralph? One shot, straight to the moon?" He pointed to the moon again. "The Kramdens?"

It took a few moments but recognition lit the emerald eyes. A slow smile lifted the corners of her lips.

"The Honeymooners. That old show—I've seen the reruns."

Old show.

"Um, 'reruns'? Do you mind explaining that one?"

She blinked. Twice. It was beautiful to watch, but he felt like a bug under a microscope. The look she gave, as if trying to decipher his intelligence, was penetrating.

Resisting the urge to clear his throat, he waited.

And waited.

Finally she shook her head. "Television was a pretty new thing in your day, wasn't it? I mean, it was just beginning, right?"

"We still had a radio in every house, almost. Some places were lucky enough to have a television set. And if you knew someone with one, you'd just go to their place to see the shows. I was always too busy to do much watching, but I liked the Honeymooners. Ed Sullivan, too."

Shelby ran a hand through her hair. She lifted her eyebrows and gave him an apologetic shrug. "I don't know how to tell you this, but every house—like, *every* house—has a set in it now. Most, more than one television, so people can tune into different things."

So progress meant that people preferred their own company to sharing time with others? An interesting, if disheartening, tidbit.

"I'm still not clear about the rerun angle."

There was no telling how long he'd be stuck in this indeterminate state, but as long as he didn't see an end date to his presence in the mortal world, it wouldn't hurt to learn as much as he could. It might be one inconsequential bit of knowledge that would open the door to the Pearly Gates. For all he knew, St. Peter ate those dreadful sandwiches while he hopped from television to television in his Technicolor heaven.

"It's not really an angle. It's more a thing, you know." She rubbed a hand on her cheek. "Sorry. You don't know, that's why we're having this conversation. Let's see if I can explain…say a show is an oldie but goodie, the networks repeat the old shows. That way, people can see their favorites more than once. And I'm sure the executives make a bundle on showing things that they don't have to produce, just rerun."

She was serious. It wasn't a gag.

"You're not pulling my leg, are you?"

Shelby shook her head. "Nope."

"So people now have so much extra time that they watch the same things they've already seen?"

"Right. Kind of like reading your favorite book over again, just because it was so good the first time."

He'd never been much on formal schooling. The

educational system had only ever been a drag in his life. But he appreciated a good book. Reading a book a second or even third time because the story was so life-changing was logical; seeing the same television show more than once wasn't. No matter what anyone said, nothing could compare to the written word when it came to bringing entertainment to the masses. Nothing.

Society didn't seem so advanced that they had cleared extra hours for wasting, but it sure sounded like that's exactly what was happening. Criticizing the current way of life—or anything else—wasn't his style, so he kept his thoughts to himself.

"So you've seen Ralph and Alice?"

A nod.

He pointed to the moon. "Look familiar?"

She leaned back against the seat, turned her face to the sky and smiled. "It does. Beautiful, isn't it?"

"It pales by comparison to your beauty, Shelby."

A sudden intake of air when she swirled to face him. Her eyes were wide. It felt as if she saw right into his soul, as if she held his heart in her hand.

They were scant inches apart. He leaned in, and her eyelids lowered. Ever-so slowly, he closed the gap between them. If she wanted him to stop, she had time to pull back or push him away.

She did neither.

He put his mouth on hers, startled by the heat in her lips. All these years, he'd been starved for contact.

Her lips opened, and he flicked his tongue inside her mouth. Sweet. Soft, sensual. She was all that—and so much more. She was the oasis, the life-giving force that made him feel almost whole again. Her tongue slipped into his mouth, swirling against his and sending a wave of heat to his core.

He wanted her. Oh, how he wanted her. Every bit of him screamed for every inch of her. Arousal like none he'd ever experienced sent his heart and mind into a tailspin. The car hummed around them, and the breeze cradling them in the moonlight was rose-scented.

It made no sense—but nothing had made sense for twenty years.

She moaned, the sound of her desire filling the small space.

"I need you." He put a hand on her neck to bring her closer but she jumped.

Shelby stared at him, her eyes round. Her lower lip quivered.

She looked as if she'd seen…shit, as if she'd seen a ghost.

And she had.

She whispered, but he caught the word. If his heart still beat, it would have instantly stilled.

"Cold…"

Chapter 26

Sleep was an elusive bedfellow. Shelby tossed for hours, looking for release from the continuous emotional chaos that refused to quiet. When the big, oak grandfather clock in the hallway chimed four, she gave in to the night and rose. Fighting wakefulness was tiring; better to give up on what was not going to happen.

She sat on the window seat, wrapped a wash-worn patchwork quilt around her shoulders and put her forehead against the glass. Its chilled surface cooled her, a welcome relief to the overworked head.

The temperature of the glass reminded her of Joey's touch.

The moon was high. So white it was nearly blinding, it lit the yard from corner to corner. The low, mournful sound of an owl in the distance. Shadows from tree branches formed a haphazard grid on the grass.

It looked like a giant spider web.

Apropos, given she felt like a fly tangled in a series of webs. No way to get out, no place to hide, and the only hope for release a slow, certain death.

Not the happiest of thoughts to run through her mind in the middle of the night.

She closed her eyes. Even without the distraction of the world around her, she was confused. No, confusion was too tame; it was much more than that. More than even what came upon her after her mother's passing.

Now, day mixed with night. Grief wrangled with academic success. Sisterhood tied her, in part, to an emotionally abusive relationship. And a gift pulled her into a maelstrom between life and death.

After last night, the line between living and dead was even less defined.

Joey Martinetti, the ghost of the Cobra's past, had kissed her. Under the moonlight. In that miniscule car where she was the only one who could see him. Speak with him. And, she now knew, touch him.

If she wasn't sure she wasn't crazy, she'd think she'd lost her mind.

It was a kiss like no other. Tender, sweet and passionate, all in one. Now, hours later, her body responded to his touch just by reliving the memory of the moment. But he was cold, too. So cold…

The deep notes of the Westminster melody chimed the half hour. In bed or out, she couldn't calm her mind.

The quilt fell to the floor in a puddle when she stood. She didn't even look down. No need to turn on a light. The moon made the walk across the room to her bath an effortless glide. She reached into the shower, turned the handle and adjusted the spray. Not too warm. If the day was to begin, she needed every bit of energy she could muster, and that included a semi-cool shower.

Her panties and nightgown landed on the soft bath mat.

Tile beneath her feet. Water raining onto her head. In between, a woman whose exterior concealed commotion. She lathered her hair, rinsed, and slathered on a generous dollop of coconut-and-pineapple conditioner.

Oatmeal scrub on her body, even on her face. Gentler around the eyes, but stringent enough that energy chased the sluggishness from her pores.

The last rinse, she twisted the water handle until the spray dousing her was near-frigid. She stood there until her heart nearly burst before turning off the shower and grabbing a towel.

She wrapped a second towel around her dripping hair, then walked into her closet.

The Physical Education building opened at five every day, a courtesy for the jocks who trained before classes. This morning a Greek would infiltrate their ranks in an effort to burn off some energy and clear her mind.

Hopefully, it would work. If it didn't, she was in trouble. There was no Plan B to fall back on—and right now, her life felt as if it might not get straightened out until she got to the end of the alphabet.

Chapter 27

Their heads tilted back. Eyes closed. Their legs out, ankles crossed, they sat with their backs against the base of a huge maple. The leaves fell, a shower of orange, yellow and red against the green grass.

It was a decidedly peaceful spot.

"Not bad for a couple of wanderers, is it?" Alfonso held a hand out, palm up, and caught a yellow leaf. He twirled it between his fingers. "Always liked this time of year."

The colors reminded Joey of heaven, but he kept the thought to himself. He hadn't shared what he'd seen, and he wasn't sure he was going to.

"Yeah, it's pretty. But a little sad, too."

"How so, amigo?" He tossed the leaf onto the grass, where it blended with the others already fallen. "This the season you passed?"

"Nah. July—a hot day. It was a perfect day, actually…except for the dying part." He pushed the memory aside. "Now? All the trees and flowers giving it their last energy before they close down for the winter. It just always struck me as bleak, that's all."

If he were still alive he would be putting the Knucklehead and Cobra in storage. A garage behind his place sheltered both from snow while he drove the runabout Ford he kept for winter use.

"I understand. Where I'm from, we didn't have

trees like this. A lot of cactus and scrub brush, but no towering maples to drop this cascade of color." He fingered an orange leaf, running a thumb over the veins. "The desert is not nearly as welcoming as this place."

"Never been to a desert. Born and raised in the northeast, where leaves fall, maple sap runs, and snow buries." These twenty years, he'd never thought to drift far from this area. The car tethered him, an invisible thread. "How'd you get from the desert to here?"

"Nothing to keep me there anymore. When I died, there was a wife, but she's long gone. I wandered around for—well, for a long time. Then I heard your loneliness so I came here."

"Heard me?"

Alfonso had removed the wide-brimmed hat he always wore and placed it on the ground. Now a finger of sunlight touched the deep brown cap of curls on his head. "That's not what I said. It was the loneliness that drew me—an almost real draw that I couldn't ignore. It's not like there are a lot of us around, so I didn't mind coming to this side of the country. A welcome change, really."

"So you felt my presence?"

"A good way to put it."

"Alfonso, how did you die?"

The other man looked up from the leaf he'd been examining. "You sure you want to know?"

"Yeah." He swallowed around the trepidation pushing the next words from his mouth. "And I've never told anyone how I died. I, ah, hell—I need to tell someone."

"Fair enough." He stared off into the distance, and Joey knew he was seeing past the scene before them.

Where his companion went, there were no maples. No hills on the horizon or birdsong from above. "It was the thirtieth of October, Eighteen Ten. The battle of *Monte de las Cruces*. Rugged territory. Pine forest. We were young. Inspired by the talk…fueled by the idea of throwing off oppression." He stopped. Shook his head. "We sacrificed much and gave everything."

"Mexico gained its independence, you know. So whatever happened in battle wasn't in vain. Your cause was won." Joey remembered enough about history to speak the comforting words with confidence.

"The cause, yes. But I should never have been there. Maria pleaded with me…we were married only three weeks before I left." He turned and gave an apologetic shrug. "What can I say? I was on the flank that took the worst of it. Many lives were lost."

Being cut down in battle must have been brutal.

Then, the obvious hit him.

"You regret your actions, don't you?"

Alfonso chuckled. "That's putting it mildly. If I listened to my bride, I would have lived a long, happy life. Maybe had grandchildren to bounce on my knee. And I would never have brought sadness to that fine-looking woman—which is ultimately the worst thing a man can do, hurt the woman he loves."

There was nothing more to say, so they sat for a few minutes. Birds sang. The breeze was warm, with a hint of apple.

"Your turn, amigo. And I want to know how that car is connected to the event, so don't go easy on the details."

Fair was fair, so he ordered his thoughts and told the whole, unfortunate truth.

Chapter 28

"I know it happened, but it's still hard to believe." He scrubbed a hand across his chin. "It was fast, just an error in judgment. Stupid, really."

"Can't be any stupider than leaving a beautiful young woman crying in bed to go march around with a pack of unwashed men."

That was a good point. With renewed determination, Joey began again.

"I never ran with a crowd, but I wasn't a total loner. I had friends—not many, but a few. We'd drag race near the reservoir. They'd come to the bar to hear me play the piano, although I know there were times they were just there for the free beer I sent to their table. Sometimes we would catch a movie. You know, ordinary stuff."

Alfonso nodded. "Ordinary for your time."

"Yeah." It wasn't an exciting life, but it was enough.

"So what happened?"

He took a deep breath. "I screwed up. I paid with my life, but that's not the worst of it. The other guy? I think he's still paying, and that's got to be a million times harder."

"Look, you're the one who said he wanted to share the story, but so far I haven't heard anything. You're dancing around like a mouse on a hot ledge. I'm not the cat who's after you, so if you want to keep it to yourself, that's fine."

The idea that he'd left so much damage behind ate at him. He couldn't hold it inside anymore.

"No, it's time to tell someone." He cleared his throat. "We knew one guy had a drinking problem, but he kept it under control. Most nights, one or two beers, tops. This particular night, he drank way too much. We all watched it. No one stopped him."

"Hard to stop a grown man from hurting himself. Not something you should carry around on your conscience."

That was the truth, but not his.

"Independence Day. There'd been a parade. And a barbeque in the park. Everyone was there. Lots of food. Too much beer. I had to play that night, so I ate a lot of chicken and grilled corn, but only had two cold ones."

He could see it all in his mind. Hear the music from the bandstand. Smell the smoke from the grill pits.

"Just tell it. You'll feel better once you get it off your chest."

His chest, right over his heart, throbbed. A stab of memory, so vivid he sucked in a fast breath.

Alfonso couldn't know, could he?

"We headed to the grassy spot where we'd all parked our cars. He was too drunk to drive, so I left him sitting on his car's bumper. I walked toward the Cobra, figuring I'd circle back and pick him up."

He heard the engine in his head and was pulled back in time.

"I should've known he'd try to drive. The Fire Power engine in his Chrysler was some big Hemi and man, did that thing roar. Rumbled, almost. I nearly made the Cobra…I was so damn close. I saw it, had the key in my hand…but I heard the car. I tried to head him off before he got to the road; put my hands up and stepped into the lane. I thought he'd stop when he saw me."

Alfonso whistled. "Been kicked by a mule many times but even the orneriest animal is no comparison."

"When I turned, I crouched a little—just anticipating the impact at the last second. The hood hit me square in the chest. The last thing I remember is flying through the air with this agonizing pain above my heart."

"Almost instant, then?"

Joey shook his head, trying to drive off the memory. "Yeah. There was only one heartbeat between alive and dead." He met the other man's gaze. "It was my fault. I should've taken his keys, but I didn't think—I just walked away and let a guy wreck his whole life over one bad decision."

"Wait a minute. You're the one who was killed, but if I'm hearing this right, you're taking the blame? It doesn't make any sense."

"Don't you see? I let him get into the car even though I knew he was loaded. He wouldn't have hit me if I'd taken the keys. And his whole life has gone to hell because of me."

"I'm not following you. How do you know that?"

Joey closed his eyes and leaned his head against the tree. A leaf fell onto his shoulder but he left it there.

"Because I saw him. He's the drunk who lives next door to Shelby and her dad." The last words barely made it past his dry lips. "One of my best friends, and I didn't keep him from making the mistake that wrecked us both. A hard thing to live with—even when you're dead."

Chapter 29

An hour of solo racquetball was just enough to get rid of excess energy. The accommodations in the gym weren't luxurious, but they were clean, so Shelby showered a second time in as many hours.

The locker room wasn't crowded, so she pulled her backpack out and put it on the bench beside her as she dressed. Bra and panties first, then she stuck a hand down into her gym bag. It closed around the plastic container so she grabbed it.

For a long moment, she held the egg in her hand. After last night, she doubted she'd ever look at a pair of pantyhose the same way again. Pushing aside the memories she'd just worked hard to erase, she twisted the egg. Pantyhose popped out, a tangle of buff-colored nylon.

She scrunched one silky leg, inserted her toes, and wiggled it up to her calf before doing the same with the other. She stood, twisting like Gumby as she worked the pantyhose into place. A last tug, and a little jump, settled them around her hips. The elastic snugged against her waistline, she sat back down on the wide wooden bench.

"Such a hassle, aren't they? I hate those things, such a drag to hop into, and then I usually get a runner before I've had them on an hour."

Shelby turned as the other woman slipped into a

pair of lavender hip hugger panties and a matching bra while they talked.

"Caro, I don't remember seeing you in the gym."

"I don't think you did, and I didn't want to bother you."

Shelby stood and slipped her arms into the light blue button-down oxford. It had survived being in the gym bag without getting too wrinkled. "You wouldn't have been a bother. Really, it's good to see you again."

"I'm here a lot. Before class and most evenings. You play racquetball, don't you?"

"Whenever I can." Her short acid-washed denim skirt buttoned up the front. It was tight-fitting, showed her slender waist well, and was undoubtedly one of her favorite pieces of clothing. The go-to skirt, worn so often it was soft. "But I have early classes, so I don't make a habit to get up before daybreak to work out. It was nice, though—a lot less busy than after classes."

"Yeah, I like the mornings better. Less craziness." She sat on the other side of Shelby's backpack and began to pull on argyle knee socks. "I'm here a lot, like I said, so if you ever need a partner…"

This morning she'd gone solo, smashing the ball against the wall on her own. At first, it had been fun, but it didn't take long before she wished she'd been playing with someone.

"I'd like that. I don't think my friends will get up at this hour, but I'd like to do this more regularly. A good way to start the day." She rummaged in her backpack for a piece of paper and pen. She scribbled her name and number on it, then handed them to the other woman. "Give me your number, we'll keep in touch."

Caro gave her a slight smile as she slid her legs

into a pair of Jordache jeans. She put her information on half of the slip of paper and handed it back.

She put the scrap into the front pouch of the backpack and zipped the bag closed. "You're obviously back at school. How's your sister? She was sick, wasn't she?"

Caro's eyes clouded, and her lower lip trembled.

Oh, no.

Instinct made Shelby put a hand on the other girl's arm and give a reassuring squeeze.

"My sister didn't make it. Goddamn leukemia...I hate that damn disease!" A tear slipped from one eye. It was dashed away by the back of a hand before she stood and zipped her jeans. She stuck her head into a blue sweater and tugged it down, jamming her arms in the holes with so much force it was a surprise the sweater didn't rip. "Sorry—I-I guess I'm still kind of raw about it."

Shelby stood, walked around the bench, and put her arms around Caro. She held on when the other began to cry, rubbing her back the way a mother would do. The wave of tears was like a sudden downpour—hard, but as quick to end as it had begun. When it subsided to sniffles, she took a pack of tissues from her gym bag and pressed them into the other's trembling hand.

Her knee-high brown Frye boots were in the gym bag, at the bottom, so she took her time getting them out. A few moments to compose was a gift she'd been given so often, it was freely bestowed now.

"I'm sorry—" Caro would have gone on, but Shelby cut her off.

"No, I'm sorry you lost your sister. But don't ever

apologize for showing love or emotion. It's okay to grieve…I know. My mother passed not too long ago, and I'm still in shock over it."

A vigorous nose blow. "Was it a surprise?"

"No. She was sick. We knew she wasn't going to make it. But none of that matters. I was shocked when it happened, and honestly I think I may be for the rest of my life."

Her boots zipped up the inside of her legs so she slid them closed and concentrated on putting her things into her gym bag. The other woman was still sniffling, and if she broke down again, it would probably mean they'd both be crying. The day already had a hard start to it; she'd rather not add to it by blubbering.

"Carlie got sick fast but lingered, if that makes sense. I wish it had happened without so much suffering, that she'd gone before it ate away at her." Caro was busy collecting her gym clothes and putting them into a lavender duffle bag. "I hate it that I even think that, that she should have gone sooner. But what happened, what I saw, what she had to go through—it was so horrible."

"It sucks. But I know your sister—like my mother—would want us to go on. Laugh. Live. Have fun." She zipped her bag. "Play wild hard racquetball early in the morning when we're the only two fools awake!"

It brought a giggle, so she added, "Hey, are you still interested in Greek life?"

Caro met her gaze and nodded. "I am. But the last rush parties were this week. I, ah, I just didn't get my act together fast enough to go to any. Sorry."

The last event was a formal. Since she'd partially

rushed last semester, maybe the sisters would agree to consider her if she attended the dinner.

"Stop apologizing." Shelby stood, shouldered her back pack, and reached for the gym bag. It wasn't half as heavy now that the boots had been exchanged for Nikes. Caro grabbed her stuff and stood, too. "Listen, I think you need some sisters. We can never replace Carlie, but we're a family—and family is important. This weekend we have one last dinner. Think you can make it?"

It looked as if a fresh torrent was about to erupt. Caro opened her mouth but was too choked up to speak, so she nodded. It was enough.

They left the locker room together. In her heart, Shelby knew the Omicron Kappas were gaining a sister who would be an asset to the sorority. They'd be able to fill the gap in Caro's life as well. And that—respect, love and friendship—was the foundation of Greek life.

Chapter 30

The day seemed to have extra hours in it. Without sleep and the time at the gym, Shelby felt as if she were running on fumes. She hit all her classes although she would've loved to curl up somewhere quiet and take a nap.

One of her psychology professors pulled a pop quiz. Another time, it might have gone badly, but the topic was phobias, and she'd been so intrigued she'd read the chapters twice already.

Agoraphobia, claustrophobia, and arachnophobia were particularly fascinating. A couple of Greek events, held every spring, might be hard for someone with any of those issues, so she was determined to recognize an aversion in anyone the next time they took place. They didn't mean to frighten potentials, but unless they were aware of a problem it was impossible to prevent a scare.

Tania waited for her as she exited the quiz. It was the first time they'd seen each other all day.

Shelby greeted her with a quick hug. "I hope you're ready to sit front and center with me in Hemingway, sister. I just had a quiz and am in a foul mood. There, I've admitted it, so you can't say you haven't been warned."

They walked side by side through the wide corridor. Their lit class was in the building, so there was no need to hurry.

"Warned? You can't scare me with a little grumpiness."

"It's more than a little, believe me."

Tania raised an eyebrow. "A visit from your monthly friend? I've got Midol if you need it."

She waved the offer away. "I wish it were that simple. No, not my 'friend'. Just no sleep and a pissy mood. Nothing, really. Change of topic: How is your day going? Fill me in, please."

A sigh. Then, the left hand, engagement ring sparkling, waved through the air between them. "My day? Why, it's wonderful…"

The singsong way the words came out, so Doris Day-ish and perfect made them both giggle. Which was exactly what Tania intended to happen.

"Holy crap, when do the little fluttering birds appear with ribbons dangling from their beaks?" She looked up, toward the tiled ceiling ten feet above them. "Cue the birds, right?"

"I can't help it if I'm riding high on love."

Shelby poked her in the side with her elbow. "Hmm…is there a glass slipper in this somewhere?"

Tania giggled. "Better than a big pumpkin, don't you think?"

"Much. But who needs ugly sisters?"

"Stepsisters."

"Whatever. You don't want to annoy your Greek sisters, princess. We're the ones who are already fighting over who's going to be your bridesmaids, remember?"

Nothing had been mentioned about where or when the wedding would take place, but that didn't stop everyone from guessing. And wondering. And planning a bridal shower, sister-fashion.

"Let them fight over that." They stopped three lecture halls down from the literature hall. Tania reached out and took her hand. "There's really only one question that matters—well, it matters the most. I don't mean the bridesmaids aren't important, it's just that—" She nearly crushed Shelby's hand when she grinned. "Damn, but I'm making a mess out of this, aren't I?"

"I don't have any idea what you're talking about. I am, however, wondering if the engagement thing is clouding your mind. A fog in there, maybe? Between the ears?" Teasing came so naturally between them.

"No fog." She shook her head, then took a deep breath. "I'm trying to ask you to be my maid of honor, but I'm royally screwing it up. So, will you? Be my maid of honor?"

Shelby squealed. She swallowed the end of it when heads turned in their direction. They hugged, their backpacks and purses getting in the way.

"Of course I will! Oh my God, I hoped you'd ask me—but then I thought you might want one of your sisters—your real sisters, I mean—so I told myself I'd be a bridesmaid—oh, no! I'm babbling, aren't I?"

They laughed, then. The chaos around them fell away, and for one magical moment there was only shared happiness.

"Fine pair we are." Tania waved a hand in front of her face, chasing away the joyful tears threatening to fall. "I can't ask, you can't answer. Who knows if we'll get me down the aisle in time to say 'I do' to Chad?"

"Don't worry, you'll get there."

"Yeah, I will." She wiped a tear from beneath her eye with a fingertip. Meeting Shelby's gaze, she added,

"And I hope you remember to ask me to be your maid of honor when you get married. That's the way this whole deal works, okay? You wrangle me to the altar, and I get a chance to do the same for you."

She nodded. Her throat was tight, her mouth dry and it was impossible to reply.

It seemed highly unlikely she'd ever walk down an aisle. In fact, she was pretty sure she'd never do it.

"Let's get to class. I want to sit in the front."

Tania understood without her having to say another word.

"Yeah, as far as we can from the creep who'd love to get you to the altar."

"Not happening, sister. Not with him, anyway."

They went inside, where spots were already filling up.

"It'll happen." They put their bags on the floor beneath their seats right in the first row. They were so near the professor's desk they could have reached out and touched it with their toes. "But not with an asshole. You deserve a nice guy, Shelby."

"Don't we all." She averted her eyes when the next wave came into the hall. Turner was among the crush of bodies.

Tania leaned close and whispered, "He's not nice. I'm sorry, but that's the truth."

She sighed. "I know."

Chapter 31

Shelby gave the professor a small smile of apology and excused herself from the lecture hall. She moved as quickly as possible and made sure the door did not slam behind her.

Maybe it was the lack of sleep. Or early morning workout. Tania's exciting news, even. Whatever it was, she was tired to the point of almost falling asleep as Hemingway was discussed just inches from her desk.

Time to get out and walk for a minute.

The ladies' room was empty. She went into a stall and did her business. The pantyhose weren't as clingy as they'd been hours ago, so she pulled them up without the extra little hop. She flushed, opened the door, and walked over to the long counter.

As usual, the sink area looked as if people had been bathing in it. Puddles of water and blobs of soap bubbles were everywhere, including on the mirror. She stood a foot back, leaned over and washed—all without getting the front of her skirt wet which was a minor miracle.

With dripping hands, she turned toward the paper towel dispenser and stopped short.

Joey, that heart-stopping grin on his face, held out a towel. She took it, dried her hands, and tossed it into the trash.

"Make a habit of hanging out in the women's

restroom?"

He shook his head. A faint blush stole across his cheeks, making him even more difficult to resist.

"No, not my thing." His color deepened a shade as he added, "And I just want you to know, I stayed outside until I heard you flush. Just in case you're wondering."

Shelby swallowed a giggle. "Well, that's something, I guess."

They stood close, but not touching. The air between them felt charged.

It took every ounce of willpower she possessed to keep from leaning forward and kissing the man right on the lips. Her gaze dropped to that mouth that beckoned her. She remembered how tenderly he'd kissed her. And, how one kiss ignited a flame that still burned.

Closing her eyes, she shook her head. "Do you realize that I've begun to wonder if I'm crazy?"

His voice was soft, nearly a caress. "I'm sorry."

She opened her eyes and met his gaze. Shook her head again, but this time without regret. "No, don't be. This week…it's been…I, ah…"

His tiny grin sent shivers to points on her body that hadn't shivered this way before they'd met. "A helluva birthday week, huh?"

"You have no idea." She inhaled, then released the breath slowly. "But meeting you has been…how do I say this? It's, ah…"

"Interesting?"

"To say the least."

Mind now swirling, she studied his face for a sign of what hid behind those dreamy eyes. A thrill shot up her spine, her body intimately aware of the attraction growing between them.

"About what happened…Shelby, if I was out of line, I'm—"

It was clear he was about to apologize. There were so many things in her life already that made her sorry, she couldn't stand the idea of adding one more item to the long list. A sorry life was no life.

She had to stop him, so she did what she wouldn't have guessed she actually had the nerve to do. Leaning forward, she brought her face to his and pursed her lips. Her heart hammered double time, knowing how skillful he was with that mouth.

As their lips met, the heavy door opened behind them on a burst of female chatter.

The touch was so brief, it was nearly non-existent. Shelby tried to compose herself and smiled when she got odd stares from the two who walked past her into stalls. She must have looked like a lunatic, standing in an empty bathroom kissing thin air.

Chapter 32

"Holy cow, you could run interference for the football team. I'm impressed."

Tania waved the compliment off. The ring on her finger caught the late-day sun and sent a shower of light.

They were out of breath when they reached the parking lot so they leaned against the front fender of Tania's car. As soon as the bell rang, they'd bolted past the professor in a blur that was nearly comical. They hit the exit hard, pushed, and practically bounced off the door frame getting into the corridor.

Neither stopped to see how closely—if at all— they'd been followed. Theirs had been a run to freedom, through the lecture hall, across the grass and into the parking lot.

"No biggie. I just wanted to get you out of there before Mr. Fathead caught up to us." They looked around. The post-class flood had begun to exit the building. "We've got to go. Where's your Cobra? I'll drive you to it."

"Not here. I took my old car."

"What? Are you nuts?"

"I hope not." The question had been tumbling through her head since she'd received the race car.

She managed to avoid Turner, who seemed to be waiting for her wherever she went, all day long. It was exhausting peeking around corners and ducking into bathrooms and empty lecture halls to avoid him, but she'd done it.

The scramble had given her time to consider a few things. Well, one thing. Not exactly a thing…but not precisely a person, either.

She had to share the news about Joey with someone. There was only one person who she was pretty sure wouldn't insist she have her head examined. She hoped.

"Why on earth would you drive your old clunker when that pretty little thing is at your disposal?"

She glanced at the crowd. They were still near the building but wouldn't be for long. If she was going to divulge, this was the time.

"Look, you've got to swear you're not going to tell anyone." She waited, but Tania just furrowed her brow and stared. "I mean it—swear you'll keep my secret."

"Really? As if I'd tell anyone anything you tell me in confidence?" An insulted huff. Then, when Shelby opened her mouth to insist, she said, "Fine. I promise. Although you didn't need to make me—the cone of silence is part of the maid of honor privilege."

If she wasn't so stressed, she would have laughed. The cone of silence, from an old-time television sitcom they watched.

Oh, right. Reruns. The thing she'd tried to explain without real success.

"Okay, here goes nothing. The car? It has a ghost."

Tania didn't bother to stifle her amusement. A snort. "A ghost?"

"Look, I know it sounds crazy. But there's a ghost in the car, a hot guy named Joey. He's, ah, he's pretty amazing and I, well…"

A hand shot in the air between them. "Hold up. Just hold the hell up." Tania met her gaze before she raised one perfectly-tweezed eyebrow. "You're telling me there's a ghost—a hunky ghost named Joey, of all things—in that sports car your dad just bought for you?"

She nodded. The crowd was coming closer. "Yeah, that's what I'm saying."

"Why didn't I see this ghost? I was in the car, remember?"

"Remember how you said you felt something? *Something*? Maybe it was *someone*?"

"Oh." Tania put her hand over her lips. Her eyes widened. "It did feel as if we weren't alone. I was nervous about saying that, so at first I kept it to myself."

Turner and two of his brothers were headed toward them so Shelby backed up. Her old car was parked two spaces over.

"You were right when you said that. When you felt it. I wish you could meet him, he's—well, he's something else. Listen, I've got to go—but don't forget, you promised not to say a word!"

"My lips are sealed!"

She hurried to the car when Turner called her name.

As she backed out, she saw Tania doing the sister-two-step, holding him back by talking and waving her arms in front of him. Anger showed on his face as she turned around and drove off.

She'd heard that he spent last night with Heather. Bad news for Heather, having a jerk like Turner Walker in her bed, but good news for Shelby. It didn't feel nearly as bad as it should have, divesting herself of a boyfriend just before all the best parties of the semester.

Suddenly, being single had a new sparkle to it. And it was a sparkle she could live with.

Chapter 33

It was just her luck that as she parked by the curb her neighbor chose that precise moment to stumble out of his pop-up camper.

Ignoring the stumble would have worked, but he fell. Flat on his face. And didn't get up.

She disregarded the goody-two-shoes conscience screaming inside her head, urging her to go pick up the guy. Offer assistance. Get involved when all she really wanted was to be left alone.

A long moment passed. She held her breath, hoping he'd move.

"Shit."

She heaved open the big, heavy door. It felt like a wall against her shoulder but she pushed it wide and got out.

"Hello?" She called, using her best I'm-a-good-neighbor voice. "Hey, are you okay?"

No answer. No movement.

Wishing to put an end to a crap day didn't make it history any sooner. She'd learned that already, having tried to wish weeks after her mother's passing away. Time had its own agenda, and moved at its own pace—even when those enduring hard times wanted it to sail by.

She released a resigned sigh and crossed from one property to the other. Now that she was closer, she saw the evidence that had been hidden by the row of bushes separating the lots.

Beer cans littered the grass near the camper. Crumpled food bags, either thrown or blown by the wind, gathered beneath the pine picnic table. Crushed cigarette butts were everywhere. It was a miracle the guy was still alive, if this was the kind of life he was leading.

"Hello?" He didn't move so she raised her voice a notch. "Hello—are you okay?"

Grumbling, and a burp.

Thank goodness, he wasn't dead. One ghost in the neighborhood was enough.

Shelby went closer, forced herself to squat beside the man. She'd never been this close to him before. Theirs had been a wave-over-the-shrubs kind of relationship. Less complicated, that way.

He certainly was a mess. Long, greasy hair. Body odor mixed with stale cigarette smoke wafted off him in waves. Over it all, the sickly sweet smell of old beer.

Hops gone bad, she thought.

"Hey, I think you should get up." She put a hand on his shoulder and shook. As usual, he wore the ratty t-shirt. It was threadbare and stained, with a tear along the shoulder seam. "If you can. Here, do you need some help?"

He lifted his head. Shook it like a dog shaking water from fur. Got to his knees, pushing up with a grunt. Another burp brought his face up.

Her heart lurched. His eyes were bloodshot and red-rimmed. The scruff covering his chin was longer than was fashionable. But more than the physical signs he displayed, the hopelessness in his light blue eyes caught her attention, grabbing her emotions and tugging.

She put her hand out, and he took it. She helped him to his feet, steadying him when he swayed a little.

"Are you okay?"

He shook his head. "Not really, no."

"What can I do?" She wondered if she should call for help. Or take him to the hospital. "Is there anyone we can call? Do you have family?"

He didn't answer right away. Rather than push, she waited. The sun's rays were warm even as it fell toward the horizon. All things considered, there were worse places to spend a few silent minutes.

The words were softly spoken, but she heard them.

"I have a problem."

If he hadn't been so disheveled, she would have put her arms around him. His sadness was overwhelming, and the urge to comfort him was huge.

But he could get the wrong idea. Her track record with men had been pretty crummy recently.

"Hey, we all have problems. That's nothing to feel bad about."

He heaved a big sigh. "I, ah, have a drinking problem." Waving a hand to the crushed beer cans, he added, "Beer. It's my downfall every time."

The situation called for a response, and she was at a loss.

She said the first thing that came to mind. "Cookies. I can hardly walk past a bag of Chips Ahoy without lifting a couple. They get me every time, too."

A small smile when he met her gaze.

Funny how they found common ground. Wobbly, but at least it was something.

"Well then I guess you understand, don't you? I, ah, I fell off the wagon. I was doing real good—man, I thought I had it this time—but, damn, I took that one first sip and goodnight, Louise, that was all she wrote."

Now that he'd begun to speak, the words came in a rush. A beer-infused cloud. Every time he exhaled, she nearly got a contact buzz.

Shelby took one step backward, just to put a little distance between them.

"Listen, is there anyone we can call? Someone to help you get back on the wagon?"

He ran a hand through his hair, scowling when his fingers got trapped in the tangles. "I let myself go all to hell. I'm so ashamed."

Now she did put a hand on his shoulder and gave a gentle squeeze.

"There's no reason to be ashamed. We've all got problems." She paused, recalling the house next door looked prosperous and happy but was empty and miserable. A lump formed in her throat but this wasn't about her so she swallowed and focused on the man beside her. "I think life's about learning how to get up after a fall. You're up, and that's all that matters. Let's get you some help so maybe you won't fall down again. What do you say?"

He nodded. "I think you're an old soul, Shelby, that's what I've got to say. Your daddy must be real proud of you, grown up to be such a good-hearted woman. I've got my sponsor's number inside the house. One call, and he'll be right over. I just have to say, 'it's Simon, and I'm in trouble'—that's our phrase for him to come quickly."

She took two steps toward the house. When he

didn't move, she said, "Come on. Let's call your sponsor. When he arrives, I'll leave."

"You don't have to stay—I know you must have something better to do."

Reaching out, she took his hand in hers and held on tightly. "Nice to finally meet you, Simon. I want to stay. And no, I don't have anything better to do. Until your sponsor arrives, I'm visiting my neighbor—and I'm thinking I might be doing more of that in the future."

"Thanks. I really lost it this time." As they walked toward his house, he leaned close and whispered, "I think I saw a ghost yesterday—and not just any ghost, either." He paused and shook his head. "Looks just like a guy I knew a long time ago…"

Chapter 34

He never thought he'd be near the guy responsible for his death but life—and death—were funny sometimes.

When Simon stumbled from the camper and planted his face on the ground, Joey cringed. Simon hadn't aged well and didn't look the way he had decades ago, but it was him. Joey was sure of it.

Shelby was an angel, running to help when she saw him fall.

Watching her push through to the other property brought a clench of emotions. Desire. Frustration. Anger.

Damn it, why did he have to find the love of his life after death? It made no sense—and was completely unjust.

"You've got excellent taste in women."

He turned just as the scent of peanut butter and bananas swept up his nose.

St. Peter polished off the last of the sandwich. Licked three fingers. Pointed to the other yard. "I can see why you can't help falling in love. She's a beauty."

"They let you out of heaven?"

Today he wore a white jumpsuit with rhinestone eagles across the shoulders. Attached to the back of the collar was a cape. A quick sweep down revealed the boots were red, with TCB across the toes again.

"Let me out? Are you serious? You do realize I'm the gatekeeper, don't you?" He shook his head so hard a lock of black fell across his left eyebrow. "And don't ask me why but when I see you've got a pocketful of rainbows but don't know how to cross a bridge over troubled waters, I've got to step in."

They looked back to Shelby and Simon. She'd helped him to his feet and was gesturing toward the house.

"Why is it that I'm stuck here watching the woman of my dreams tend to the man who killed me?"

"I don't have an answer to that—I'm just the messenger, remember. Not the big guy."

Simon was so disheveled his fingers caught in his hair when he brushed it back.

Watching sent a stab to Joey's heart. Sure, he was dead, but he'd never sunk to such depths. No man should be so downtrodden.

"He never got help for the drinking, did he?"

St. Peter shrugged. "Doesn't look like a rags to riches story, does it? He carries a heavy burden, with no one to help him make it through the night."

"I'm so sorry." Anger melted as Shelby walked his old friend into the house. She'd put a hand on his shoulder, and while he couldn't hear her words, the tone was comforting. "I thought I was the one who got the shit end of things, but he's had it worse."

"You never know what someone else deals with unless you walk a mile in their shoes."

"I wish I could do something to help him."

St. Peter glanced over his shoulder. "Poor Simon, he's saying 'I need somebody to lean on' but until your long legged girl with the short dress on came along, he's been out of sight, out of mind." He met Joey's gaze, a quick, but serious, study. "First, clean up your own backyard, Joey. Then, patch it up with him, and there'll be peace in the valley—for everyone."

Never one for crossword puzzles or word games—he had been too busy tickling the ivories and running around on his bike—he had no idea what the flashy saint meant. How could he help the other man realize he'd already been forgiven when Simon couldn't even see him? Peace in the valley—when and how?

Peace.

Alfonso.

Now was his chance.

"Listen, there's another guy stuck here."

St. Peter looked behind him. To his right, then his left. Finally, he glanced up at the clouds, sending the big wave of thick black hair across his brow. He lifted one corner of his upper lip and snickered. "I was raised on rock, where seeing is believing…put the blame on me, but I'm not finding king creole—or any other guy."

"No, not here, exactly. I mean, he's here, in this between-dead-and-alive limbo. Like me—only longer than I've been here. Actually, he's done this ghost bit for at least two hundred years." Joey pushed a hand through his hair and wondered if it was even worth it to ask at this point. He'd learned that some things, like gaining access to heaven, came—or didn't come—in their own time.

What could it hurt to try?

"Alfonso. He's here, too, and while I'm glad for the company, it seems he should get a pass through the Pearly Gates. He's dragging regrets that should've been forgotten so long ago…it's just a shame, is all I'm saying. Can you help him?"

He endured a long, hard stare. It was a moment that, had his heart been beating, would have been heart-stopping in its intensity.

Finally, a nod. "I know Alfonso. You might be right; time to make the world go away for the guy. Just send the long black limousine, help him forget the hard memories, and give him a pocket full of rainbows. You're a good friend, to think of him this way." He pushed up his right sleeve and glanced at a gold wristwatch. "Funny how time slips away. I've got to get back."

In the adjacent yard, they had disappeared into Simon's house so he turned to face the well-heeled saint.

"That's it? Don't you have any words of advice? Anything to help me?"

A fog emanated from the ground beneath the red boots. Swirling colors, rising in a cloud.

"Hey, you're not a puppet on a string. If you've really got a burning love for the lady, consider a little less conversation and a little more action. Grab your dream, Joey. It really is now—or never."

Chapter 35

By the time the sponsor arrived, the last of daylight was long gone. A cool breeze blew, sending a wave of goosebumps across Shelby's body. She shivered, wrapped her arms around her middle, and walked past the camper and its alcoholic litter. Pressing through the shrubbery, she was once again reminded that while her life was far from perfect, it was a lot better than the lives of many others. Simon's, for one.

She made a mental note to remember to pop over from time to time with a plate of cookies or just to say hello. The poor guy was lonely, looking for a friend in the bottom of a beer can. Maybe when he'd cleaned up, she could help him find some kind of volunteer work. There was a Big Brothers team in town; they were usually looking for mentors.

Simon's claim he'd seen Joey and that he was someone he'd known in the past niggled at her. She did a quick calculation in her mind. Alcohol ages a person, but it was definitely possible that if Joey were alive he would be as old as her neighbor.

It was something she could ask him about the next time he showed himself.

She opened the back door to the trusty old car she'd parked just a short while ago and removed her back pack. Instead of shouldering it, she grabbed it by the top loop and set it on the car hood.

The Cobra was parked in front of the garage door. Nestled in the exact same way it had been on her birthday. Then, she'd had a wave of disgust roll over her when she looked at it. Now, some regret.

She'd been hard on the car. Harder still on the guy who came with it. Hardest on herself, for expecting she wasn't capable of mastering a new skill. She'd felt in a funk for so long she'd convinced herself that was her lot in life. That she belonged—deserved, even—to occupy the rut she'd created for herself.

Well, that was behind her. Seeing the sponsor, hearing the way he worked with the broken soul next door, shot home the truth. She didn't plan to ever forget what she'd learned.

It's a choice to be happy or sad. A conscious decision to either be broken down by circumstance, or lifted up with the power to overcome obstacles. There was no crapshoot about life. If something was off, it was because she allowed it to be. If she was treated badly, it was because she let that happen. If she was miserable, it was because she chose it over happiness.

The time for pity parties was past. They had lingered way too long.

Shelby ran a hand along the line of chrome at the rear of the Cobra. Tomorrow, and every day until the first snowstorm, she was going to drive the car. And she was going to enjoy the hell out of the experience.

A hand on her shoulder made her heart jump.

She hoped Joey would materialize and had been about to get in the car to see if it would bring him but this was better. Outside the car, there was more room. And she needed all the room they could get because she was going to entice him to kiss her again. If he did, this time she would keep her stupid observations to herself.

So what if he was…ah, a bit on the chilly side? There were worse things than that.

"Hey, I'm glad you showed up." She turned, wishing she'd put a fresh slash of gloss on her lips.

But it wasn't who she hoped to see.

"Turner!"

Her gut clenched when she saw the anger flashing in his eyes.

"You sound surprised—and I thought I was getting a hero's welcome." He was so close she could practically taste his breath in the air between them. The sweet smell of pot shrouded him like a cloak.

She tried to take a step back, but her legs bumped the rear of the Cobra. Between the car and his body, she was pretty much pinned in. Nowhere to run.

Nowhere to hide.

"I have to go inside. My…ah, my father's waiting for me."

He shot a glance at the dark house. His face twisted into a sneer. "We both know better. He's not home."

"You need to leave." She kept her voice steady. It was difficult, considering she wanted to scream at him to get the hell out of her driveway. "Now."

He crossed his arms, a stubborn pose she'd witnessed many times in the past. He was getting set to dig in his heels.

"So I guess you were expecting someone else?" He looked at the deserted street. Back to the house. To the neighbor's yard, where a light had come on in one of the downstairs rooms.

"Go home."

"Who were you expecting, Shelby?" He leaned so

close spittle flew from his lips onto her cheek. "Seeing someone on the side? Is that it?"

Holding her temper would have been wise, but in that moment she understood how a bull felt when the red cape waved in his direction.

She squared her shoulders, just to let him know she wasn't going to be intimidated. Not by a jackass who couldn't even act human.

"You should know about that." She waved a finger in the air, punctuating every word. It took all her self-control not to poke him right in the chest. Over the spot where his heart should be—but wasn't.

The effort of talking seemed too much for him. Confusion clouded the eyes she once thought were dreamy. Well, she'd learned a few things from this fraternity fool.

They were together longer than they would have been if they weren't part of sorority and fraternity life. The hard feelings left behind after an inter-Greek breakup took a long time to heal. Shelby had never wanted to bring that to the sisters.

Even if it did cause a rift, she had to break away. The less time spent with the maniac in her driveway, the better.

She did the unthinkable, then, and poked him in the shoulder. "I know about you and Heather. Don't think you put anything over on me, because you didn't. I know—and I don't care."

Turner squinted, surveying her through heavy-lidded eyes. His lips formed a straight line. What had been anger now showed as barely-restrained fury. A blood vessel throbbed in his right temple.

"You don't care? Is that any way to treat your

boyfriend? We're pinned, damn it!"

"You're not my boyfriend—and you can have the stupid thing back." She put a hand on her collar, but the pin wasn't there. She'd left it in her gym bag with the rest of her jewelry when she'd changed. "I'll give it to you in the morning. Now, get out of my driveway!"

Too late, she saw him reach for her. He grabbed her by the wrist, his grip so tight she nearly screamed. When he began dragging her across the driveway, she protested.

"Let me go—damn you, let me go!"

He pulled open the Shelby's passenger side door and, taking her by both wrists, practically lifted her off the ground and shoved her in the car. "I'll let you go when I'm good and ready. Not before!"

Chapter 36

If she thought she could manage and not kill herself, Shelby would have jumped from the moving vehicle. The idea repeated itself, running through her mind like a song playing in a loop on a cassette tape but she couldn't bring herself to do it.

Once or twice, she'd put a hand on the door handle, scanning for a possible safe roadside landing spot. Every time, she'd backed off. To begin with, they passed a lot of rural countryside on the way downstate. If she jumped, it had to be somewhere that she could find help. Or where somebody would see her and offer assistance.

Even if she did jump, what would stop him from hauling her back into the car? She knew him well enough to know that when he had an idea in his head—even a self-serving, depraved and potentially damaging one—there was no convincing him to reconsider. In Turner Walker's world, he was never wrong.

The first few minutes had been a mistake. She'd yelled, hoping he'd release her if she got angry, but all that did was piss him off. The guy couldn't write an essay, but he sure as hell had a powerful backhand.

Her jaw felt as if it had met the business end of her sorority pledge paddle. Her face throbbed, but she kept silent. She had no intention of giving him any satisfaction. He'd meant to hurt her, and he had, but she wasn't going to let him feel strong by showing weakness.

The guy was a bigger asshole than she'd imagined.

When they neared the city, he took a joint from his shirt pocket. Lit it, pulled in a long, slow toke. Holding his breath, he held the marijuana cigarette out to her, motioning for her to take a hit.

Shelby turned her face to the window. She knew what would come next.

As if on cue, he blew a stream of smoke right into her face. Most of it hit her left ear and hair, but enough passed her cheek that she was suddenly in a cloud.

She waved a hand, but it really didn't make a huge difference. The windows were rolled up, and she doubted he'd let her roll one down.

"You'll loosen up when the shit gets into your head." His words were slurred. Soft. Almost gentle.

"Let me out, Turner." She wasn't stupid enough to scream again. Despite his dreamy tone, he was a loose cannon. Keeping her voice even, but not pleading, she tried to appeal to whatever morals he had left. "You don't need to do this. You don't want me so please, just let me out."

His fingers tightened on the joint. Ashes fell onto his thigh, but he didn't look down.

The second drag wasn't as long as the first. The smoke drifted from between his lips when he spoke. "You don't know what I want."

"That's right, I don't. But please, let me out of the car."

They were in traffic, the line between country and the edge of the city crossed once they were over a narrow bridge. The club was near the outskirts of town, so the influx of traffic wasn't unbearable. Unfortunately, the landscape had turned from empty stretches of flat land to dark warehouses. Every street looked deserted. And dirty. Not at all a friendly spot to run for help.

"You'll have a good time tonight. You'll thank me tomorrow."

Tomorrow was going to bring a lot of things, but gratitude for what was happening now was not one of them. Things like pressing charges, policemen, and lawyers—along with expulsion from the university and who knew what kind of mayhem within the Greek community. Nowhere did she see thankfulness for the terror and bodily harm he had chosen to inflict upon her.

If she was going to get out alive, she had to stay smart. Focused. Determined. And in control of her emotions.

It was a stretch to call the venue a club. More like a small warehouse, a squat, one-story building with brick walls and a flat roof, it was in the center of a dark street in a lousy section just outside city limits. It was doubtful the place would pass a code enforcer's inspection.

He pulled into a paved lot beside the building. A crudely-designed billboard hung by a length of wire off a high metal fence. It listed parking rates, so when they reached the attendant Turner already had cash in hand. He passed it through the window. Adding a twenty, he asked the guy if there was a spot close to the entrance.

For the extra cash, there was, so he parked. As he shut the engine off, he tossed the last of the joint onto the floorboard near his feet.

"Cool ride, Shel. I'm gonna drive this more often."

Hoping for Joey hadn't made him appear. She was, apparently, on her own. Summoning more bravado than she felt, she shook her head. "I think not."

"I don't give a shit what you think. You're mine, and this car is part of the package." With the speed of an eel, he reached for her hand. When she wouldn't give it to him, he growled, "Come on!" and wrapped his fingers around her wrist.

He put his mouth against her ear. "Do anything stupid, and I'll kill your old man."

Blood turned to ice in her veins. She hated him like she had never hated anyone in her life. In that instant, she hated him even more than that god-awful Lou Gehrig's disease that killed her mother.

He pulled his head back. A satisfied smirk turned the handsome face ugly. His gaze searched hers, and when she didn't flinch, he nodded.

"Good. We understand each other. Now let's go have a good time."

Chapter 37

Joey witnessed the abduction. He was right in the middle of it, actually. Well, beside it. Shoulder to shoulder with Shelby, he felt every shiver pass through her body. He hoped she felt his presence—even if she deemed him cold—and that her shaking wasn't due to fright.

Damn it all, he wished she'd never gotten into the car.

But she hadn't had a choice. Her struggles had been in vain, and he wasn't able to help her. He wanted to, but psychic energy was a tricky thing; one shift in the wrong direction and it could take out a building. His power was strong enough that if he miscalculated and hit her instead of the jerk—well, he couldn't take that chance.

He'd waited all day for her return. Passed the afternoon by hiding the last of Simon's beer in the bushes so he wouldn't hurt himself. He didn't see how it could change circumstances if he drank himself to death.

After St. Peter departed, he lingered, ready to make a move when Shelby stopped beside the Cobra. It was time to try to make things right with her. Hopefully find a middle ground between them.

But Turner appeared like a bad smell. Sudden and nasty, and while he stood watching the creep had kidnapped Shelby.

And there hadn't been a damn thing he could do to stop it from happening.

He paced the driveway, considering the options. He had to rescue her, that was clear. But showing up in the car and startling her so much that maybe she did something that would get her hurt—or worse—was out of the question.

He might as well be impotent.

He'd never understood the word before, but now there was no doubt in his mind. And it had less to do with sex than people realized. This pervasive helplessness was too much to bear.

Shelby's father pulled up by the curb. He got out of the blue sedan, briefcase in hand and shoulders pulled low. The man looked worn out from the outside in, as if he diminished a little bit each and every day. Somehow, he had to find a way to help the guy, make him see he wasn't the one who had died. Maybe a support group…

But first, to bring Shelby home.

The backpack on the hood of the car caught the other man's attention.

Joey waved his hands in front of her father's face. "She's gone! That jackass Turner threw her in the Cobra and drove away—we've got to find her!"

But the elder man didn't listen. Or see. Or understand.

Shelby was certainly the only one with the ability to communicate with him.

Fortunately, her father sensed something amiss. He called out, "Shelby? Honey, are you here?"

Moving quickly across the grass, the banker called again, but of course he didn't get an answer. As he went into the house, lights came on, flooding the yard from the windows.

Her dad would phone the cops when he didn't find his daughter. Wouldn't he?

Chapter 38

Bodies pressed tight against each other, beer spill making the floor slick. The band's apparent be-loud-if-you-can't-be-good philosophy, combined with blue-and-red strobe lights, had given Shelby a whopper of a headache. As in, she could barely think, her head pounded so hard.

None of it seemed to have an effect on Turner. He belted out lyrics when the spirit moved him, held her wrist when she refused to hold his hand, and acted as if this were the best date in the history of mankind. Every time he bought a beer for himself, he got one for her. She deposited the full glasses on any available surface. Once, she intentionally let a glass slip, hoping to draw some attention to herself, but there was so much broken glass on the wet tiles nobody even looked her way.

The first time her captor had loosened his grip was in a crush just outside the men's room.

"Don't move." The words were slurred. A rough shove against the wall near the sign, then he went through the open doorway. The instant his back disappeared, she wove her way through the sea of bodies.

"Excuse me. Please, excuse me." Using her elbows, she none-too-gently cleared a path.

She tripped when she got closer to the exit door. A bouncer uncrossed his arms and caught her by the shoulders. "Hey, careful."

Whizzing past him, she made it to the sidewalk. It had been dark when they went inside, but now it was midnight dark, and raining hard. She pressed against the building's brick front so the black metal fire escape hanging from the second floor gave her some cover. She scanned the street as she weighed her options.

No money. No idea where she was. No clue where to find the nearest train or bus station—or even a phone or police station.

An instant to consider was both too long and long enough.

She turned to the right and sprinted for the intersection. A glaring traffic light beckoned.

Two cars were stopped when she made it to the end of the street. She raised her hand and waved, ready to run into traffic. Hopefully one of the two would take her away from here.

"Help! I—"

She hadn't heard him behind her but she sure as hell felt his hand wrap around her arm and swing her around.

"No!"

Turner's face was rain-slicked and inches from her own. He smiled, leaned down, and kissed her as he put his arm around her shoulders and pulled her close. A wave for the occupants of the two cars, whose light had turned green. She heard tires on wet pavement as the only hope she'd had for escape drove into the night.

She didn't make him drag her back. He was much stronger, and even if she struggled, there was no one around to see them. The chance of a Good Samaritan happening along was next to nothing.

"I told you not to move." He snarled into her ear when he released her lips and began to walk. Their pace was brisk, despite his heavy breathing.

A bolt of satisfaction at having made him run shot through her. Turner hated any physical activity that didn't involve drinking or sex.

"Let me go home."

They neared the club. No one was on the sidewalk, but the door was wide open. The rain couldn't muffle the sound of the horrible music. It filled the air, a fingers-on-blackboard annoyance that made her jaw clench.

"Please—the music, it's too loud. My head hurts, Turner." Appealing to whatever bit of humanity lurked inside the drunken, agitated man beside her was a gamble. He might insist on driving—in fact, she was certain he would—and that could be even more dangerous than staying put.

She wished she could devise a plan to get the keys from him. So far, no burst of inspiration on that front.

He planted a sloppy kiss on her temple, sending a stomach-turning beer breath curtain into her face. "You need to loosen up, is all."

"I need to go home."

They reached the club, and he headed straight for the door. Shelby planted her feet, refused to walk, but the sidewalk was wet and she slid. Turner's grip held her upright, saving a fall.

"Hey, c'mon. Let's have some fun." The puzzled gaze would have made him endearing if he hadn't forced her to do his bidding. "You know I love you, don't you?"

They stood beneath the fire escape on the deserted

sidewalk.

Ironic, that a man had finally uttered the three words every human, male or female, yearns to hear, yet they did not impact her the way she expected. She fought the tears burning the backs of her eyes.

Bringing love into this horror of a relationship was wrong. So wrong, it stung.

"What about Heather? Do you love her too?"

He furrowed his brow. A slow smile as he shook his head. God, but he was handsome—but like a shiny red apple with a worm inside, his looks concealed the truth of the man.

"Nope. Heath-Hea—" He burped and nearly got sick. She backed up as he swallowed, then waved a hand in front of his mouth. A drunken grin as he said, "See? Not in love with her. Almost made me puke—she's just a bed warmer, Heather is."

The comment made her ill. How could she have ever thought she cared for this shallow, miserable excuse for a human being?

"I want to go home, Turner. Let me go—I'm calling for someone to pick me up."

He went from cuddly to nasty in a heartbeat. "Don't be such a bitch, Shelby. You'll go home when I say so. Not before."

Chapter 39

Frustration grew as the hours sped by. Every minute that passed meant Shelby was in peril. Each second wasted by the ineptitude of humans was one second more that she could be abused.

Joey could barely control the emotions stirring within him. He'd never felt anything this strongly before. Not in life. And certainly not after his death.

The Carmichael house was lit up like a Macy's store display the day after Thanksgiving. Every light in the place was on, including the ones in closets, the basement, and garage. Long fluorescent bulbs spilled yellowish pools onto the back deck and patio.

He wanted to scream. Didn't they see she wasn't hiding? Putting on all the lights, searching inside closets and under beds—as if she were a little kid playing hide and seek—was a waste of precious time.

Probably because he was a big fish in a small pond, Carmichael's insistence patrol cars come to the house added to the light display. Two cruisers, sirens silent but light bars on, sent blue and red circles across the scene. Neighbors stood on front lawns, figures emerging from darkness with each swirl.

"We can't file a Missing Person's Report yet." The cop tapped his pen against his notepad. Chewing his lower lip, he added, "It's just too soon."

His partner came in the front door, past the empty

rooms, and into the kitchen. His black shoes squeaked against the polished floor. "Nothing outside. No sign of abduction. No indication anything, ah, disturbing took place on the premises."

Hands clenched at his sides, Carmichael's gaze darted from man to man. Despite the navy-blue, three-piece suit, white shirt and red tie, he looked ready to kill someone. His eyes were wide and his jaw clenched.

The first one made the rookie mistake of holding his arms wide. "See? Your daughter probably just ran away. Kids do that."

Lightning fast, the notebook was knocked from his hand. The older man took a step forward, putting less than a foot between himself and the startled young cop. A hand on the butt of his gun, holstered at his waist, was the only response the second cop made.

"Look, asshole, my daughter did not run away. She would never, ever do that. And she's not a 'kid', some random young dope head who has no respect for her father. I'm telling you, something is wrong."

"Calm down, sir. Please, calm down." His voice took a stern note. "And don't ever touch an officer that way again. My notepad should not be on the floor—an officer's belongings—"

"Screw your belongings! Don't you understand? My daughter is in trouble. She would not leave her bag like that. Her wallet. Keys. Everything—damn it, *everything* is in that bag. If Shelby's not here, something is wrong. Very, very wrong. Damn it, help me!"

Joey swallowed the scream he knew no one would hear. He looked around for some way to alert them. Some way to give them a clue.

A miniature water globe sat on top of the ivory wall phone. Inside, the city skyline. Twin Towers. Chrysler Building. Statue of Liberty.

He crossed the room, stood directly in front of the telephone, and closed his eyes. Concentrated energy, until it felt his head would explode. Then, he pushed with his mind.

The water globe flew onto the floor, hit, and burst like a grenade. Pieces of plastic scattered around a slur of scenery-littered water.

"Holy shit!" The cop who'd misspoken reached around and picked up his notepad. The top page was damp, splashed by the explosion. "What made that happen?"

The second cop took a step back. His complexion was pasty, and the hand on his gun butt was so tight his knuckles were white.

Carmichael stepped forward, knelt beside the mess, and extricated the cutout of the Empire State Building. He held it between two fingertips, turning it over for a long, silent moment.

"My wife gave this to Shelby just before—" He paused, cleared his throat, and looked toward the back door. Outside, light shone in the darkness, a warm glow on the patio stones. When he met the other men's gazes again, he gave them a half-smile. "It was just before she got so sick she couldn't leave the house. This was our last family trip before my wife died. Shelby is in the city. And I know she's not there because she wants to be. Call it Father's Intuition—but please, help me. I lost my wife; I can't lose my daughter. I just can't."

Chapter 40

Turner didn't make the same mistake twice. He didn't return to the restroom.

When she said she needed the ladies' room, her captor waited outside the door. Her hopes fell when she saw there was no window in the three-stall, closet-like space.

She wasn't sure Turner wouldn't barge into the bathroom and drag her out if she lingered, but she didn't care. She'd pleaded for her freedom. Tried being soft-spoken and done some screaming. She'd threatened and cajoled. Nothing worked. And now, there was no escape from the smelly room, so she did something she hadn't done in so long it felt strange to do it now.

Chatter in the room, coupled with the mind-numbing stage music, effectively concealed her words.

She closed her eyes and screwed up some courage.

"God, it's me, Shelby. I'm not real good at this anymore, and we both know I'm still angry with you over what you let happen to Mom, but please help me out here. I'm trapped. I've got to get away, but how?"

"Babe, it's me."

Not God.

Shelby's eyes opened the instant she heard his voice.

"Joey!" Her arms went around his shoulders and

she crushed her body against his. He was cool, despite the hot stickiness of the club, but she didn't care. "Oh, I'm so glad to see you! Turner—he's got me—"

"I know." He ran a calming hand down her arm when he pulled back. A fast assessment. His gaze lingered on the spot where she'd been backhanded. "I'm going to kill the bastard."

"Forget him—help me, please. I've got to get the hell out of here!"

Again, he trailed a hand down her arm. When he reached her hand, he grabbed and held it.

She winced, biting back a scream as she withdrew her hand and cradled it to her chest. It had been crushed so hard by Turner that she wondered if every finger wasn't broken.

"I'm going to kill him for doing this to you!"

"It'll be okay." She wanted to cry, but there wasn't time. She'd already taken too long. Turner would be in to get her any minute now. "Please, help me get out of here."

"I can't do much." He plowed a hand through his hair. "If I try to get to him, I could hurt someone else. I can't risk it—taking down an innocent with my power. I'm sorry."

Regret tinged his words. It tore at her heart.

"I understand. No one else should suffer because I suck at choosing boyfriends." She shook her head. Turner had not been a boyfriend in a long time. "No, I'm bad at losing creeps, is what I am. What the hell am I going to do? How can I get away from him?"

"Hang on. Help is coming—your father and the cops, they're on their way. Just hang on, and stay put." He put a hand on the wall behind her and leaned close.

The scent of spearmint chased off the stench of the toilets. "They're running the plates on the Cobra. It's a hard car to miss, and they know you're in the city. They're talking to the scumbag's brothers about his plans for tonight, so it's just a matter of time before they get here. I'm with you—just stay put, okay?"

She nodded. His eyes were points of light in the darkness. She wasn't alone, and for the first time since the abduction she believed she'd make it out alive.

"Okay. But I hope they hurry—he's out of his mind!"

Chapter 41

As she emerged, Turner held out a glass. Beer sloshed over the side when he waved it at her. Rather than end up wearing it, she took it.

"Drink, Shel." His was already half empty when he put it to his mouth and drained it.

"Not thirsty." She had to shout to be heard. "I want to go home."

The scowl that twisted his face would let a casual observer think his glass had held battery acid instead of Budweiser. A wide ledge ran along the wall. It already held empty bottles and glasses. Adding his to the others with one hand, he unceremoniously grabbed hers with the other. The move sent a splash onto her skirt.

"Damn it, Turner—you're a pig. You know that? An absolute pig!"

He chugged her beer. Wiped his mouth with the back of one hand. Dropped the glass onto the floor and grabbed her hand. This time, she resisted.

The crush of bodies made pulling away impossible. And he tightened his hold so drastically she was almost certain her fingers were broken.

"Stop—you're hurting me!"

She scrambled to keep up when he wove through the crowd. A crush of bodies dancing to the music made her feel like a ball inside a pinball machine. Bounce off a leather jacket, bump into some guy's shoulder, get her ass pinched by an unseen hand. It was heart-pounding chaos.

Earlier they'd seen two fraternity brothers and their dates. Both couples had been sober, and expressed their opinion that the band was a bomb and the club a dive. She suspected they were long gone.

No familiar faces as they moved through the place. Not one.

At least Joey knew where she was. And help was coming.

Song lyrics—not the ones coming from the sound system—infiltrated and ran like a loop through her mind.

The truth of it was that there was nowhere to run. Nowhere to hide. Nowhere…and no one to help her.

Appealing to Turner hadn't worked. Waiting for him to pass out hadn't done it, either. And he had been mellow for a while but was getting agitated again.

He's taken a hit of something, she thought.

"Hey—you're hurting me, damn it!" Shelby twisted, slapping his bicep with her free hand while she tried to get away. His grip was so strong that all she did was pull her fingers further into his, but he did stop and turn to face her.

The eyes that met hers were frighteningly bloodshot.

"What?" Turner grinned. Tried to kiss her. When she turned her head so he only got her neck, he bit her ear.

"Stop!"

She raised a hand to him, but he caught it. Now he held her close, pressing himself against her with a drunken leer.

"You're mine. Act like it."

He'd turned into someone she did not know. Chilling stare. His gaze penetrated, and not in a good way. The sneer that pulled his lips tight was mean. And hungry.

For the first time, fear turned her insides cold.

"Turner, please…" The words came on a whisper as her knees turned shaky, and she knew that even if he could hear her above the din, it didn't matter. His heart, whatever was left of it, was hard. There was no mistaking what he had in mind when he pushed his hips against hers a second time.

"No need to beg, Shel." The diabolical wink stilled her heart. "I got just what you need."

He spun. Dragging her behind him, he pushed through the crowd toward the front door. It wasn't the worst walk she'd been forced to take—the steps from limousine to graveside would always be the most agonizing of her life—but it was a close second.

Every hour that passed she wondered if this was how the night would end. It was the thing she prayed wouldn't happen but as they left the club behind and he strode toward the car, she realized her prayers had fallen flat.

There were lights in the far edges of the parking lot. The spot where he'd parked was closer, in a dark area. Had they wanted privacy, it would have been perfect. He should have been staggering, he'd had so much beer, but something fueled him because he moved so swiftly across the space she practically had to jog to keep up.

They reached the Cobra. Shelby pulled hard, ignoring the pain shooting up her arm from the hand that felt crushed.

"Let me go!"

He dug in his pocket for the keys. She yanked his arm when his hand emerged, and the key ring fell to the asphalt.

"Damn it! I dropped the keys—"

When he leaned down, she pushed him. Hard.

"What the—" Turner landed on one knee. He whirled, pulling her hand. "Bitch!"

She pushed again, and he tipped sideways just enough for her to bring up a knee. The move wasn't perfect, but the self-defense instructor would have been proud. She nailed him on the chin. The back of his skull thudded against the passenger door so hard it scared her—but only for an instant.

Turner released his hold so she bolted. The black top was rain-slickened. Her boots had three-inch heels and she slipped but she found her center just before she went down. It all happened in a heartbeat, but it was as if unseen arms caught her, set her on her feet, and gave her a quick shove forward.

Behind her, footsteps, coming fast.

"Shelby—damn it, Shelby—"

By some miracle, a car drove by just as she ran into the street. Turner was right behind her so she didn't stop. She'd rather be hit than subjected to his fury.

The blaring horn was the last sound she heard before her right hip made contact with the Chevy's hood. Her feet left the ground at the same instant the tires on the big car squealed. Another thud, and screams.

Time seemed suspended as she flew toward the far side of the street. Instinctively her hands came up to cover her face.

All of her senses were heightened. A soft light surrounded her. The air lost its wet chill, suddenly warm against her cheek. She tasted blood, and the smell of beer spilled onto her skirt intensified. And the strong scent of spearmint washed over her.

In her ear, a familiar voice. "I've got you, babe."

Chapter 42

"Hold on. Help's coming."

Shelby hadn't moved since he set her down on the cracked sidewalk. He'd tried to make it a soft landing, but after he got creamed by the car, it wasn't as simple as all that. They were lucky he was able to lift them up and over the hood. If he'd been mortal, they'd both be crushed beneath the heavy automobile.

And the crowd would be waiting for the coroner instead of an ambulance.

He wasn't going to dwell on any of that. Now, he needed to focus. Concentrate on the life still within her and use all of his power to keep her alive.

Joey bent nearly double, cradling the still form against his chest. Her breathing was slow, but regular, and a hand between her breasts told him her heart was beating. If only her eyes would open. Just once, so he could see the soul in their emerald depths.

A few people had come close, but he waved them back. Until medics arrived, no one was going to touch her.

He wouldn't allow it—if his love couldn't sustain her, nothing could. It was an unquestionable truth. Somehow, he was the link that bound her to earth and kept her from transcending.

It defied logic, but he was certain it was a fact.

Her eyelids fluttered.

"Babe, can you hear me?"

Sirens, distant a minute ago, grew louder. The ambulance was close. Their time was at an end.

"Joey." His name came on a whisper. She smiled—then her face twisted in pain. "It—oh!"

"Don't speak, just hang on. You'll be fine, I promise." It was the only vow he could make, and it came straight from his heart. "Shh…here they are. Doctors, to help you."

The ambulance skidded to a stop on the wet pavement. Onlookers retreated to the other side of the car behind him. He was aware of clusters of people, but until the medical team ran forward, he did not move.

When it was clear he could do no more, Joey placed Shelby on the ground and touched a kiss to her forehead. A kiss of respect. To protect…and sustain.

The team put a blood pressure cuff on her arm and started an IV drip. They began to take her vitals.

She was in good hands, so he turned and scanned the crowd.

He saw the bastard standing next to a lamp post and was on him in an instant.

It would have taken no force to topple the drunk, but Joey let him have it. The shove sent him sprawling on the slick concrete in front of the club.

"You almost killed her!"

Walker shook his head, as if trying to clear it. He rolled over, got to his knees, and tried to stand.

Rage consumed Joey. He placed his foot on the small of the other man's back and pushed. Like a house of cards, Walker collapsed. A howl of pain as his nose broke just an instant before he vomited.

Joey waited until the retching stopped. Then, he

pushed the creep down one last time, making sure his face landed in the mess.

Chapter 43

Joey had no memory of the swirling vortex. No sense of movement. The transition from grimy street scene to rainbows and pearl-studded picket fence was instant.

It was a blessing, because for the first time in a very long time, he didn't feel that hot.

"Welcome to my world, again." St. Peter slapped him on the shoulder as he appeared beside the fence. As before, there were plush chairs, but this time they were leopard print with gray fur throw pillows. "Shake, rattle and roll—and have a seat."

No need to invite him twice. His legs were wobbly, and something throbbed in his temple. If he didn't know better, he'd swear it was a headache.

And a backache. And a prizewinning pain in his side.

But it couldn't be.

He sat on the closest chair. It was soft and man-eating, but his body still hurt.

He frowned. "Is this what dead feels like?"

The other man settled onto the empty chair. His blue velvet jacket, black dress pants, and starched white shirt was a change from the jumpsuits and rhinestones. Diamond cuff links sparkled at his wrists. A thick gold TCB pendant hung around his neck.

With a chuckle, he shook his head. "That's a

question for somebody bigger than you and I, but no, what you're feeling is not death."

"Then what the hell is going on?" Joey tried to push himself up but had no strength.

"Remember, in my father's house we need to stay loose." The saint looked around, as if worrying they would be overheard. He lowered his voice. "I saw your blue eyes crying in the rain. I understand your burning love for Shelby."

"They're brown." The statement earned him a puzzled stare, so he added, "My eyes? They're brown."

Rings on each finger made the hand wave solid. "Details."

In all the time he'd been dead, Joey had never been as confused as he was this very minute. Was he dead? Or was he still a ghost? And if he wasn't confined to heaven, he had to get going.

Shelby needed him. If he didn't know anything else, he knew that.

"Okay, so if I'm not dead, what am I?"

"It's funny…I'm not new at this job but at times like this, I'm all shook up. In a good way, that is." St. Peter crossed his arms and tilted his head. He narrowed his eyes and gave Joey a long, thoughtful look. When he spoke, his tone was serious.

"Joey, don't think twice, it's all right. Fools rush in where angels fear to tread, but you're no fool. She is, however, an earth angel. Cherish her. You've done your part, sacrificed yourself for love. Now, it's time to shake, rattle and roll. But remember, there's no room to rhumba in a sports car." A chuckle, and a head shake. "Enjoy every minute—you've got this second chance, but it's impossible to grant this wish again so make this count." He stood, put out his hand, and pulled Joey to his feet. The minute they touched, electricity charged the multi-colored air.

He tried to thank St. Peter, but the vortex pulled him in before he could speak.

As he headed back to earth, he heard the gatekeeper's parting words.

Return to sender...

Chapter 44

"Are you sure you're well enough? I can stay home, you know."

Shelby looked up from her book. Her father was dressed for work, but he didn't appear ready to leave.

She smiled. "Stop frowning at me that way. You're like a Mama Hen, hovering over me still. Look, the doctor says I'm fine. Go to the bank. I'm okay."

Their relationship had changed drastically these past two weeks. They were close again, in a way they hadn't been since her mother passed away. The walls he'd built around his heart had come down, and the guilt they both felt at surviving when the woman they adored had not was something they discussed. At first, there had been tears. Now, there were moments of understanding. Peace. Laughter.

"That's Papa Rooster, if you don't mind." Father sat on the wicker chair beside hers. Leaning forward, he put his elbows on his knees and clasped his hands. Threaded his fingers together, a habit he'd lost during the time when they were strangers living in the same house. "Look, it's cool if you don't want to be alone. I can take a leave of absence. I've got lots of time built up and really, I don't mind."

They'd discussed this at length, with each other as well as with the counselor she'd been seeing. Everyone agreed it was time for her to resume her life but now, at the jumping-off moment, it was clear he had second thoughts.

Healing. They both deserved it.

Shelby reached over and put her hand on his. She waited until he lifted his head and met her gaze.

"Hey, it's time. We both get to live—and laugh—now, remember? Mom's at peace; we need to be, too."

"I almost lost you." His eyes glazed. "I couldn't have survived that, honey."

She had lost him, after her mother's death, but she didn't point that out. He already knew, anyhow.

"But you didn't. And you won't." She said that, but they both realized it was a lie.

There were no guarantees. Loss was a part of life. They'd been reminded of that awful lesson again on the horrible night she'd nearly been killed.

Still, they needed peace. Today was a big step forward, for both of them. Sending him back to work with a smile on his face was her only goal for the morning, and she had no intention of fumbling.

"I'm going to class in a little while." She held up the book so he could see the title. "*The Old Man and the Sea*, discuss and analyze. You know it's one of my favorites."

He shook his head. "Your mother would be proud. She adored Hemingway, too."

She loved it that he mentioned her now.

"What can I say? Two peas in a pod." They both grinned. It had been one of her mother's favorite expressions. "And the girls waited for me to have the luncheon for the prospective new sisters. I've got to go, especially since Caro is going to be my new little sister."

"Ah, I see. Hemingway and a new little...there's no way I can convince you to stay home another day, is there?"

"Nope."

He stood, put his hands in his trouser pockets, and pulled out his key ring. He offered it on his palm. "Are you sure you don't want to take my car? Easier to get into, and all that, than the Cobra."

She closed his hand around his keys. "No, thanks. The Cobra is my car, remember? We talked about this."

"You're sure?"

"I am."

They had discussed the car, among a ton of other topics, after the night with Turner. There had been lots of tears, and they washed away so many hurts and so much resentment that she saw the car through a different light now.

He'd wanted her to feel loved, even when he didn't think his heart still worked. The Cobra was a symbol of that emotion, and something he and her mother had wanted to give her from the day she was born. It was a story told long after it should have been, but her parents thought they'd have time to live all their dreams. They thought to present their Shelby with her own Shelby Cobra together someday.

That her father cherished her enough to carry out one of her mother's last wishes took her breath away.

She would never sell the car. It was part of her now, because it came with unrivaled love.

"I'll be here when you get home from classes."

He'd said he wouldn't be working late anymore, but she wasn't sure he'd keep that promise. She didn't intend to hold him to it, so she raised an eyebrow.

Her father chuckled, jingling his keys on his palm. He leaned down, kissed her cheek, and squeezed her shoulder. "You'll see. I'll be home—with a pizza so we don't have to cook. But promise you'll be careful of that hand. I know the doctor cleared you for driving, but if it's too hard with the cast, give me a call. I'll be at my desk all day."

She had given the whole driving thing a test run yesterday. It was a challenge, but she'd done okay.

"Go to work, and don't worry about anything. I'm fine!"

Chapter 45

Taking turns one-handed was not a simple maneuver but Shelby got the Cobra into a parking spot without incident. She'd chosen the spot beside Tania's car so even if she scraped something it would be a sister's bumper and not so much of a big deal. But no bumpers were damaged so she turned the ignition off and sighed.

Relief that she was resuming life, both at home and school, made her smile.

She looked at the passenger seat.

Empty.

Another sigh.

She hadn't seen Joey since the night he'd saved her.

His presence touched her in a way that had scared her in its intensity. Now that he was gone, she was afraid she'd never feel that way again. Her heart hurt from missing him.

And there was a hole in her life that hadn't been there before they met.

A soft tapping on the window beside her head made her turn. A face was practically plastered up against the glass. The smile was contagious.

Tania opened the door and reached in to help her out before grabbing her in a hug.

"I would have picked you up—why do you have to

be so stubborn?"

"I need to do things for myself."

The words were barely out of her mouth when they were surrounded. Cries of "Welcome back!" and "We missed you!" filled the air as she was hugged by sister after sister.

When they released her, she saw there were brothers waiting to welcome her, too.

The fraternity president and several brothers had visited the hospital. Turner had been expelled from the university and stripped of his brotherhood status. They wanted her to know they were completely supportive of whatever course of action she chose to follow.

She did not want to press charges, but her father's attorney made it clear that it was her responsibility to do so. She'd given it some thought and realized he had a valid point. Being kicked out of school and banished from the fraternity was life-changing, but they were not severe enough punishments.

Shelby could not stomach the thought that Turner would do to someone else what he'd done to her, so she agreed to legal action. He'd been arrested when she was still in the hospital. Of course, his family posted bail, but there was no way they would buy his way out of the case. She was not going to drop the charges, and her attorney assured her justice would be served.

A brother removed her backpack from the car and slid it onto his shoulder. Another held out an arm, so she put her hand on his forearm and let him walk her to class.

A figure stepped out of the crowd and gave her a gentle hug. She fell into step beside her. "I'm so glad you're back. And I can't believe you're going to be my big sister. It's more than I ever dreamed would happen."

Shelby saw Caro was dangerously close to tears so she smiled up at the brother beside her. "No crying, little. Didn't you read that in the charter, that Omicron Kappas don't sniffle in public?"

Her joke had the desired effect, with the other sisters and their prospective littles joining in. Sniffle jokes began, which led to silliness, which brought them all into the lecture hall in near hysterics.

Goodbye hugs and promises to catch up on the wall later in the day were exchanged at the door. The brother deposited her backpack on a seat in the front row when Tania pointed out their spot to him.

Before he left, he said, "After class, another brother will meet you at the door, right over there." He gestured to the passage they'd just come through.

"It's not necessary. I can carry my bag, thanks."

He shook his head. "Sorry, but no. We'll carry your things and see you safely between classes, until you're fully recovered." He winked, a shyly teasing move. "Who knows? Maybe you'll see we're not all bad. And, Shelby? I'm sorry for what happened. We all are."

She nodded. "I know. And, thank you—and the other brothers. I'm sure it'll be less tiring if I don't have to lug around anything except this silly cast."

When he walked away, Tania said, "I think he's got a crush on you."

"Let him crush. I'm not interested—in anyone."

"Any word from, ah...you know?"

She was pretty sure Tania believed her about Joey. They had talked about him, and the car, for hours.

Shelby poured out her heart to her, even about missing him.

"Nothing."

"I'm sorry, sister."

"Me, too."

She felt like crying but forced a smile as the professor came into the room and did a little dance inside the door when he caught sight of her.

A few hours later, Shelby realized her first day back had passed in a blur.

Hemingway, fraternity brothers treating her like a queen, lunch with the sisters, and two more classes had pretty much wiped her out. She'd been kissed, hugged, and welcomed too many times to count.

It was all great, but as she turned into the driveway she realized the cast felt as if it weighed more than she did. All she wanted was to get in the house, relax with her father, and maybe watch the sunset from the back porch. She had homework, but not so much it mattered if she left it until tomorrow morning.

Chapter 46

"I'm happy you're driving again."

That voice. Shelby turned, praying she wasn't hallucinating.

"It's you." She'd had plenty of time to consider what she wanted to say to him. Hours to rehearse in her mind witty, brilliant, endearing speeches. Why, then, did something so ridiculous emerge from her mouth when the chance finally showed itself?

If the cast hadn't been on her arm, she would have slapped herself in the forehead with her free hand.

Her free hand...she looked down. Joey's left hand covered her right where it lay on the stick shift.

"Yeah, it's me." His eyes were as she remembered, so deep and dark she wanted to fall into them. "I mean it. I'm glad you're well enough to drive. The Cobra missed you, I'll bet."

Opportunities came and went. People, they did the same. Time was not endless—she knew that. It was a lesson learned through heartbreak, a truth of her life.

Even if she looked ridiculous, she wasn't going to let the chance to speak her heart pass.

"I missed you." When he didn't say anything, she leaned forward. "Joey, I missed you when you weren't here. And I'm sorry I said what I said, the night you kissed me."

"Don't be sorry."

"I am. I didn't think. It just came out—oh, I hate that I said that. I drove you away with my stupidity."

He squeezed her hand. "No, you didn't. You told the truth, and the truth is never stupid."

"I've felt so awful. We were never the same after that. I tried, but we didn't have time."

His gaze shot to the house. To the yard. To her father's car, parked at the curb. To her father, standing inside the front door. Simon stood beside him, a smile on his face and the ratty t-shirt gone, a neat blue sweater in its place.

Joey waved to the figures in the doorway. A return wave from her father before he turned and walked away. Simon did the same before disappearing into the house.

He gave her that little lopsided smile that made her heart flutter.

"The past is behind us. What happened before? We can't change it." He took a deep breath. When he exhaled, a hint of spearmint. "All we have is now…and a hope for years to come. I've known since I first saw you, from a distance, that I'd give anything for a chance at a future with you."

She wondered if he could hear her heart pounding in her chest. It sounded loud to her own ears. Her hand shook beneath his.

"I don't understand. Joey, you know you're a ghost, don't you? I mean, how can we have a future—" She looked down when he squeezed her hand. His touch was gentle.

Warm.

She gasped.

A sparkle in his eyes when she met his gaze. He

nodded.

"You're…" She swallowed. Leaned in close. Inhaled the sweet scent of spearmint when he smiled. "Joey? Are you…?"

The word would not come, so he nodded.

"Alive."

"But how?" Memories from the awful night slammed into her. "You were there, weren't you? The instant the car hit me—you were there!"

It didn't matter what he said. She knew, deep in her heart, that he had been the one to save her that night. All along, the doctors had called it a miracle that she hadn't been killed by the car. She'd been too busy getting well to pay much attention, even when they insisted Turner had not been hit. She'd heard a second thud against the car—she'd heard it and knew she wasn't the only person struck.

Now it made sense.

"Hey, don't pass out, okay? You father will have my head if you faint. Babe, are you okay?"

He put his hand against her cheek. It, like the one still covering hers, was warm. His forehead touched hers, for just a second, before he ran a thumb across her lower lip.

"Shelby, I know you're shocked, but I can't wait…I love you. With all that I am, I love you." His gaze was so gentle when he asked, "Please…I have to know. Could you care about me?"

He looked into her soul, and she felt his hand hold her heart. It was so pure and tender, and oh, God, it was so right. It was the rightest thing that had ever happened in her life.

A sob, pure joy and relief, tore loose from

somewhere deep inside her.

When Joey gathered her against him and held her tight, Shelby finally knew peace.

His mouth found hers. Tender, sweet and full of promise, the kiss sealed their fates. Tears of happiness slid down her cheeks and a shaky laugh escaped when he released her lips.

"Don't cry." He wiped her tears with a fingertip.

"You saved me from being killed, didn't you?"

"We need to forget that night." He shuddered. "Really, we should leave it in the past."

She already knew. She'd known all along. The look in his eyes just confirmed her suspicion: Joey, the ghost in her Cobra, had sacrificed himself for her. He'd saved her life, at whatever expense he'd have to pay.

"I love you, Shelby. I want to spend the rest of my life with you."

"My heart—you have my heart. I have to spend the rest of my life with you…"

He smiled, and the rest of the world faded even further away.

"Your heart is safe with me, I promise."

Shelby knew that. Her heart. Her life. Her future. All of it was safe, now. As long as they were together they'd be fine.

"But how? You're here—Joey, how?"

It seemed impossible, yet here he was. Warm. Solid. Holding her close.

Alive.

"It seems even St. Peter sees I'm stuck on you. So please, love me tender, babe…forever and ever."

A word about the author…

Sarita Leone loves adventure, whether it be in a distant continent or her own backyard. When she's not off exploring the world, she keeps busy writing, reading, and dancing beneath the stars.

Always a fan of happy endings, she's fortunate to have a job which allows for so many of those!

She loves to hear from readers. Easiest way to connect? Check out her Facebook page, where all the latest news hits the screen.

Thank you for purchasing
this publication of The Wild Rose Press, Inc.

If you enjoyed the story, we would appreciate your
letting others know by leaving a review.

For other wonderful stories,
please visit our on-line bookstore at
www.thewildrosepress.com.

For questions or more information
contact us at
info@thewildrosepress.com.

The Wild Rose Press, Inc.
www.thewildrosepress.com

Stay current with The Wild Rose Press, Inc.

Like us on Facebook

https://www.facebook.com/TheWildRosePress

And Follow us on Twitter
https://twitter.com/WildRosePress

www.ingramcontent.com/pod-product-compliance
Lightning Source LLC
Chambersburg PA
CBHW060930180626
46817CB00004B/1468